I dedicate this book to my Pap Pap Emilien Augustine Fernand Danel (a.k.a. Morris). Because of his legacy and leaving his hometown in France at the age of sixteen, it spurred my curiosity to follow his journey and experience France for the first time in my life. I also dedicate this book to all of my newfound cousins in France, especially to Patrick and Genevieve Warin. Because of their warm hospitality, generous sharing of family history, and phenomenal French cuisine, it inspired me to create the setting for this book. I will forever cherish the memories of discovering my Danel heritage along with the beauty of France and all it has to offer.

POINT AND SHOOT FOR YOUR LIFE

ROBIN MURPHY

CHAPTER ONE

I FOCUSED THE LENS OF MY PENTAX-K 500 AND saw the heaving, creamy breasts bobble over the pink lace underwired push-up bra. As I adjusted the angle of view to include the pouty red, plastic-like, high-gloss lips and diamond-pierced nostril, I asked myself, *why the hell am I shooting porn?*

The taped paper makeshift sign on the door read, *Hannah Mills – Freelance Photographer*, 'freelance' being the operative word. I liked doing freelance, and I convinced myself I liked living in the historic, quaint town of Sharpsburg, Maryland. I suppose it was easier to remember my glory days of playing soccer at Boonsboro High School, where I graduated with honors and then received my B.F.A. in art and photography at the Maryland Institute College of Arts, than to think of my current situation... broke.

Because of my fear of being thrown out into the world and having to get a job, I chose to go after my M.F.A. in photographic and electronic media and then became one of the boomerang kids living with my parents, George and Daphne Mills, at the age of twenty-three, with mounds of academic debt.

Fast-forward eight years and I'm no further along with my dream of being a highly respected photographer for *National Geographic* or Microsoft Corporation, bringing down a salary of fifty-thousand a year. In fact, I recently lost my second job as a clerk at the local BP station because I was late, for the fifth time, and didn't open the store for the early morning commuters.

Brittany Carson cleared her throat and said, "Are you taking pictures or just pretending? I'm in a bit of a hurry. I'd like to get these finished for my Harry."

Brittany was a petite-framed, five-foot-two, bleached blonde bimbo who got knocked up at the age of sixteen to Harry Carson, the local auto mechanic. They live in an apartment above the garage on Antietam Street. Brittany tends bar at the local watering hole called Pete's, and it was rumored she did porn movies on the side, which would account for the double D's she had implanted after the birth of her second child.

I did an imaginary eye roll and continued taking pictures for her cheesy pin-up calendar, which would probably only pay me enough to make a car payment on my used 1998 cyclone blue pearl Honda Civic.

I stood up from my squatting position and said, "I think I have enough for you to use in your calendar. So why'd you decide to do this for Harry? I mean, you've been married over six years and have two kids together."

"Because we're approaching that seven year itch thingy." She gave me that hollow look and continued, "You know that thing that guys do when they get the itch to look elsewhere after seven years of marriage? I don't plan on letting that happen. So I thought I'd give this to him to hang in the garage. He'll be able to brag me up to his customers and only have eyes for me when he comes home."

I chose not to respond, because I needed the money and didn't want to give my usual sarcastic reply to piss her off. "What a nice thing to do for your husband."

Brittany got up off the blanket and stretched for her robe. "How have you been doing since Brett picked up and left?"

I chose not to answer her question at that moment and continued to look at my camera, pretending to be doing something photography-wise, when I caught her stare out of the corner of my eye. "I'm sorry, what did you ask?"

"I asked how you were since Brett dumped you?"

"I'm doing great. Life is much better without him in it."

Brett Thomas was a guy I fell madly in love with and lied that I was a virgin when we met at the Corner Pub on Mulberry Street in Hagerstown. After three weeks, we moved in together in his townhouse on East Chapline Street in Sharpsburg, which is where I currently reside. The rent is fair, and the view of the Antietam Battlefield is magnificent.

Unfortunately, Brett decided he was suffocating and left in the middle of the night, leaving me with a recliner, a park bench make-shift sofa, a plastic coffee table, one oddly shaped, green glass lamp and a 1999 Sharp television set. He knew better than to touch the dining room set, which was a gift from my Great Aunt Dorothy.

"I thought you were going to be some famous photographer and move to the big city or something.

That's what your mom said." Brittany finished dressing in her cut-off jean shorts, tube top, and red spike-heeled sandals and casually handed me a check for one hundred and fifty bucks.

I grabbed the check and slipped it into the back pocket of my skinny jeans and said, "Yeah, well my mom says a lot of things. Thanks again and I'll send these pics to your email address. Once you choose your favorite twelve and decide which pic goes to which month, I'll design the calendar."

Brittany blew a pouty kiss into the air and winked. "Thanks again, Hannah, you're the best. I'll get back to you soon."

I watched her sashay out of my studio, which was an empty room of the vacant old theatre on Mechanic Street, owned by Diane Hall. Diane is a real estate agent for Coldwell Banker, and a close friend of my mother's, who always took pity on the less fortunate. Apparently, I fell into that category. Don't get me wrong, I'm glad to have a free space to use for my clients, but it got a little old listening to Diane's *poor Hannah* statement every time I saw her.

I had fifteen minutes before the bank closed to make my car payment, so I chose to leave my equipment as is and locked the door behind me. Jefferson Security Bank was located at the square on Main Street and only a half block away from my studio.

I was waiting for the incessant traffic to break when I spotted my landlord, Connor Barnes, and immediately ducked behind a tree, which did absolutely nothing to conceal me. Fortunately, he was busy jamming a piece of PVC pipe into his truck and didn't notice me. I was a week late on my rent and didn't feel like making excuses again, or lying that I had the rent check sitting on my kitchen counter.

I slipped through the zooming cars and darted into the bank and tried to avoid Otto Lansbury's disturbing flirtations and made the payment. Then I quickly crossed the street and decided to head over to my brother Justin's place to check up on any family gossip, and mainly hide out until I knew Connor was nowhere in sight.

I jumped into my car and drove around the block to Church Street and made a right back onto Main Street and headed east toward Boonsboro. It was only a fifteen-minute drive to my brother's place, and the view of farms and open fields along the way was always pleasant.

I turned into the Sycamore Run development and weaved around the first bend and pulled into the long blacktop driveway, which led to the split-level, brown brick and cream, vinyl-sided house. I spotted Justin trimming a lilac tree, wearing jeans, a Metallica concert t-shirt, and Timberland work boots. He's six foot three with the same dirty blond hair as me, only his eyes are brown versus my green, and he was born ten years earlier. In fact, our birthdays are three days apart, which is a bone of contention with Justin because he always felt like he got robbed when I was born.

I parked next to his Ford F-250 blazing red-hot truck, waved and gave him one of my cheesy smiles. I got out and walked over to where he was sweating and throwing dead limbs into a bucket. "So, how's my favorite brother doing?"

He casually gazed up at me and squinted at the sun. "I'm your only brother and I'm fine, but I've been waiting for your niece to get home. Between her college graduation, turning twenty-one, and her whining about getting a job, I needed something to do to keep my mind occupied."

My niece Amanda, Mandy for short, is a wild child, which are the exact words my mother uses to describe her behavior. You see, Justin got divorced when Mandy was six and had to move back in with my parents and me. It was a good thing Mom didn't work; she was able to stay at home with us.

His ex-wife (her name is never mentioned in our conversations... kind of like Voldemort) kept the house they bought and continued to run around with the neighborhood strays until she got herself pregnant and ran off with a guy from Texas.

Needless to say, she didn't want anything to do with Mandy and dropped her off on my parents' doorstep. My brother's house went into foreclosure, and the world was turned upside down for Justin and Mandy, but we all pitched in to help raise her. I was only nine when Justin announced the news that he'd got *her* pregnant. My parents said it wouldn't last and they were right; however, as time went on Amanda became very angry that her mother had just dumped her and never stayed in touch. For some reason, I became her closest confidant, and to this day we are more like sisters.

After a few years of backbreaking work, Justin started his own landscaping business, which has grown into a thriving company of fifteen employees. He was able to move out and buy the house down the block from my parents, pay for Mandy's college education, and of course float me a loan or two over the years.

I leaned over and took a sniff of the lavender flower and closed my eyes. "I love this tree. So, tell me, where is Mandy arriving from?"

"She's still over Tammy's place after a night of partying. She's supposed to get home and start helping me in the office."

"Why don't you give her the summer off? She just graduated, and you know what it's like to turn twenty-one?"

Justin got up from all fours and grabbed the bucket of lifeless flowers and shook his head. "Good old Auntie Hannah. You're always sticking up for Amanda. Look, if I don't put her to work right away to give her a sense of what it's like in the real world, she may end up like..."

"Like who...? Like me? Is that what you were going to say?" I slammed my hands on my hips and stuck out my chin.

"Yeah, exactly *like* you. You know damn well you stayed in school so you wouldn't have to get a job. You've been skating along for the past ten years. Hannah, I love you to death, but you're thirty-one and you have nothing to show for it."

I shrugged my shoulders and followed him into the garage. "I know that. I just don't like hearing someone else say it. Look, any day now someone will see my work and *bam*, I'll be sitting pretty."

"Mm-hm, well until then, I don't need you taking sides with Amanda when she starts whining that she doesn't want to go to work. She has a business degree now, and I plan on teaching her my business. If she chooses to work somewhere else, that's fine, but until then she needs the work experience. And I could use the help."

"Hey, I could work for you."

Justin dumped the yard waste into the back of his pickup truck and shook his head. "Oh no, we tried that, remember? You were never on time, and you screwed up the payroll. Face it. You're not office material."

I sheepishly said, "Yeah, I guess you're right. By the way, did Mitch ever forgive me for messing up his social security?"

"Let's just say you'd be best not to show up at the office for a while."

I heard a horn and turned to see Mandy pulling into the driveway in her brand new, pewter-gray convertible Mustang. "Is that her graduation present?"

"Yeah, I got a great deal at Massey Ford in Hagerstown."

"You always get a great deal." I walked over to the polished vehicle and shook my head. "Hello there, Mandy, aren't you looking fancy in these new wheels?"

Mandy's smile revealed well-shaped, even, white teeth, which was the result of braces at age fourteen. She was an inch taller than me, and her hair was the shade of sable, which was tied back into a ponytail with a bright pink scrunchy. The pink paisley sundress fell tight against her slender body. Another reason she gave my brother gray hair.

"Aunt Hannah, I'm so glad to see you. Wait until I tell you what happened at Tammy's place." She looked at her father and whispered, "Maybe it'd be better to tell you in private."

I fell into her opened arms and took in her Cotton Candy fragrance and squeezed her back. "Yes, I believe there are certain conversations your dad would prefer not to hear."

She reached into the back seat and pulled out a box marked *Only To Be Opened by Addressee.* "Here, Nana gave me this to give to you. It's been driving her crazy to know what it is and she said as soon as you open it, you're supposed to let them know what it is immediately."

"Who would be sending me a package?" I didn't recognize the return address, but the state was New Jersey, which is where Great Aunt Dorothy lived, who died two months ago. "It's from Jersey. I wonder if it's from Great Aunt Dorothy's estate."

Justin shook his head and grabbed hold of Mandy and kissed her forehead as he stared at me. "I don't know why Aunt Dorothy had such a fascination with you. The whole family thought she was a nut. Maybe she left you some money."

"She wasn't a nut, just a bit eccentric, and I highly doubt it's money. If it were, it'd be a check in a small envelope." I looked again at the return address and saw the words, *Andrew Gerard, Esquire.*

"Don't just stand there, open it!" Mandy grabbed the box and ran over to the picnic table and set it on the bench. "Here, I have a nail file that'll cut the tape."

I watched her slice the tape and carefully open the cardboard flaps. I leaned over and pulled away the white tissue paper and revealed a linear-striped, black and cream blanket. I lifted it from the box and held it up as it unfolded in front of me.

Justin asked, "Is it a blanket or a rug?"

"I think it's a blanket. It looks to be made of wool,

9

but it almost feels like silk." I draped it over my arm and allowed them to touch the soft fibers.

"Why would Great Aunt Dorothy send you a blanket?" Mandy looked back in the box and pulled out a sealed envelope. "It has your name on the front."

I set the blanket on top of the box and took the envelope addressed to me. I tore it open and pulled out a handwritten letter from Great Aunt Dorothy. As I began to read the words, I stopped short on a sentence that stated *First Phase Indian Chief Navaho blanket*. "She says it's a Chief Navaho blanket. Her grandmother gave it to her. She's kept it in this tissue in the box ever since. She thinks it may be worth something because she saw a similar one on the *Antiques Roadshow*, but she never had it appraised."

Justin picked up the blanket and said, "There's definitely some age to it."

"What are you going to do with it? Are you going to have it appraised?" I watched Mandy take the blanket from Justin and snuggle it around her shoulders.

"I have no idea what to do. I wouldn't know how to get it appraised." I needed to steady my legs a bit, so I walked over to the picnic bench and sat down and continued reading the letter. I read the salutation and let the paper fall into my lap. "This is crazy. What if it *is* worth something?"

"If it is, you're going to be rich, and you can finally pay back the money you owe me." Justin winked at me and grabbed the end of the blanket and ran it between his forefinger and thumb.

I suddenly remembered why I came here in the first place and knew I had to get the courage to ask Justin, again, for half my rent money. Although, with the way I wear my emotions, I could see him giving me that *you've got to be kidding* look. "Why are you looking at me that way?"

"Because you're about to ask me for money, aren't you? I can read you like a book." Justin shook his head and pulled out his wallet. "How much this time?"

I gave him my best guilty 'poor me' face and said, "I only need half of my rent."

"Which is...?"

"Four hundred and fifty should cover it."

Justin looked straight into Mandy's eyes and said, "This is exactly why I want you to start working in my office. So you don't end up like this, begging for rent money."

"Aw, Dad, Aunt Hannah is living the dream. She's following her passion."

I caught my brother's eye and could instantly read his mind, which was warning me about how careful I needed to be before I spoke. "Mandy, your dad is right. You need to get out in the world and begin to make a living for yourself. You don't want to rely on others. I think working in the office will help you understand business, how things work from the ground up. It's not a lot of fun living from day to day not knowing how you'll pay for your next meal."

Mandy's eyes were wide and revealed more sclera than normal. I knew she was utterly shocked at what I just said. "You're the one who keeps telling me to live my dream. To go after what makes me happy and live and think outside of the box."

Justin said, "Yeah, well, you need to work and make money, so you're not living inside of a box on the street. Now, let's head into the house and discuss your work schedule."

I watched Mandy's shoulders slump as she grimaced at the touch of her father's hand on her back. I knew I'd just thrown her a curveball, but I needed to respect my brother's wishes, and I couldn't completely disagree with how scary it was at night not knowing how I would pay my bills. I waved goodbye and grabbed the blanket and decided to head over to my parents. I wasn't thrilled about that idea, either, but I wanted to pick their brains on how I might find a legitimate appraiser. Maybe the blanket would be worth something, and I could finally set myself up for life. Then again, it could be worthless, and I'd wind up using it as a throw over the back of my fancy, makeshift, park bench couch. It may actually work with the throw cushions I added. Who was I kidding...? My life was a mess.

CHAPTER TWO

I PUT MY CAR IN REVERSE AND BACKED OUT OF MY brother's place and grudgingly headed down the block to my parents. The neighborhood was nice. Your typical neighborhood with cookie cutter homes in the usual cul-de-sac layout. Mom and Dad's place was just outside the development, with their back-yards facing each other. I remember Dad complaining about how, after twenty-some years, the view would change now that the old farmer, Jeb Long, was dead and his stinking, rotten, greedy kids sold the land to a Baltimore developer.

As I pulled into the gravel driveway, I could see my mother peeking through the sheer curtain. Some-thing I remembered doing every time my dad came home from a hard day's work as a mechanic at Mac Truck. The red brick ranch hadn't changed over the years, other than the trees and shrubs had matured and the shed showed more age. I shut off the engine, took in a deep breath, and then grabbed the box.

My legs felt like lead every time I approached the front porch steps, something that developed over time from hearing my parents lay guilt about my lifestyle.

When was I going to get a *real* job and when was I getting married?

I reached the gray steel door and had just made a fist to knock when the door swung open, and Mom grabbed me by the shoulders and yelled back to my dad, "George, your daughter is here... finally."

I gave her a big, fake smile and replied, "Hi, Mom, how are you? Can I at least come in and sit down before you start your usual commentary on my pathetic life?"

Mom was wearing powder blue capris and a printed cotton shirt and orthopedic shoes. Not exactly what would make the cover of *Vogue*, but nonetheless, you had to love her confidence. She was five-foot-seven, an inch shorter than me, and proportionally fit for a woman in her late sixties. It was obvious my eye color came from her, but my height came from my dad. But something I noticed recently was that my hair was almost as short as hers, which was something I decided to remedy.

"I'm not saying a thing, why do you always jump to conclusions?"

"Oh, I don't know... old habits? Mandy said you wanted me to stop by and let you know what was in the box."

"I wish you wouldn't call her Mandy, and yes, why was the box from an attorney's office? What trouble are you in now?" Daphne looked toward the living room where sounds of *The Andy Griffith Show* came from the television. "George, come in here so we can hear what trouble Hannah is in again."

I rolled my eyes and heard the television turn off and spotted a shadow against the wall as my dad strolled into the dining room. He was five-eleven, trim, gray and balding, and his left hand was missing a pinky from an accident at work. It happened when I was a baby, so I only ever knew him with the deformity, and to this day I still couldn't look directly at it.

I watched him give me his half smile as he leaned in and kissed my forehead. "Hello, Hannah, it's been a while."

"Hey Dad, yeah, I guess it has."

My mother shook her head and slammed her hands on her hips. "That's all you two have to say to each other – 'it's been a while'?"

I chuckled and leaned over for the box and set it on the top of the dining table. "This box is from an attorney's office, but it was left to me by Great Aunt Dorothy."

I saw my mother stop short and whip around as her eyes bugged out of her head. "From Great Aunt Dorothy? Why would you get something from her? I don't hear from her for months on end, then she ups and dies, and then *you* get something? She was *my* godmother, you know!"

"Yes, Mom, I know that she was your godmother and you were her favorite. I have no idea why I got this blanket."

"What kind of a blanket?" She grabbed the box and pulled out the Navaho blanket and ran her hand across the woven fabric.

I watched my dad's eye twitch as he ran his good hand over the edge of the blanket. "I think I remember seeing something like this on *Antiques Roadshow*."

"That's exactly what her letter said." I pulled the envelope out of my back pocket and again read the line about the possible value. "Can you think of any

15

local appraisers that might know something about this?"

"You could check with Melinda Hale. She owns that antique shop in Sharpsburg right behind her house." Mom carefully touched the blanket and then sat down in the dining chair. "I never knew anything about this. Great Aunt Dorothy never spoke about it. Neither did your grandmother. What if it is worth a lot of money? What will you do with it?"

"I don't know, but that's what I need to find out. I don't know if I should keep it in the family or donate it to a museum."

Dad set the blanket back in the box and shrugged his shoulders. "You sell it for all it's worth and get yourself out of that damn townhouse and make something of yourself."

"George, this is from my family, not yours. You'd sell anything to make a buck." Mom leaned on her elbows and stared directly into my eyes. I always hate it when she does that. "Hannah, you need to be smart about this. Make sure you honor Great Aunt Dorothy's request."

"I am. She told me to find out its value. It says so right here in the letter. She wanted me to have it." I got up from the chair and grabbed the box and tucked it under my arm, and then leaned up and kissed my dad's cheek. "I'll go see Melinda right away. If she doesn't know the value, she'll be able to direct me to someone who does."

Mom shook her head and bounced up from the chair and walked into the kitchen. "Do as you wish, but remember who has bailed you out of many money problems."

I caught my dad's chuckle and gave him a wink.

"Sure will, Mom, thanks and I'll let you both know what I find out." I quickly left the house and jumped back into my car. I knew Melinda was probably in her antique shop and would only be there another hour until closing. I hoped she could give me some guidance, or even appraise the blanket. She was pretty well known in the area and had a ton of contacts.

As I made the short trek back to Sharpsburg, I glanced over at the box and said out loud, "Aunt Dorothy, if you can hear me, help me find out about this blanket because if it's worth anything, it sure would help me pay back everything I owe Justin, and then I guess Mom and Dad, too."

I shook my head. What was I thinking? Why the hell was I talking to my dead Great Aunt Dorothy? I must be losing it, or maybe my hunger was causing my delirium. That's what it was. I was starving. I needed to grab a quick bite at my place and then head over to Melinda's.

I pulled into my gravel driveway and took a look at the tan vinyl-sided townhouse I used to share with my ex. It was a nice enough place. It had a red metal roof and front door and a great side patio where my shaded canopy sat. I liked to retreat there when I needed to be out in nature. It was nice to be able to zip the side panels closed so nobody could see I was in there, which was something I did when I hid from my landlord.

I looked around at my potted hydrangeas, wave petunias, and baby's breath and realized I'd better water them before they withered away. August was a hot month in this area, and we hadn't had much rain. I unlocked the door, dumped the box on the dining table, and quickly grabbed some bread and made a peanut butter and jelly sandwich. I poured a glass of iced tea and sat down in the only real furniture I had, my dining room.

As I relished in the combination of blackberry jelly and peanut butter, my mind began to drift off to a scenario of owning my own place with a studio, but before I could continue in the pleasure of my fantasy, I heard a car door slam. I quickly got up and looked out the living room window and saw my landlord. My immediate reaction was to flee out the front door, but then I remembered that Justin had lent me half the rent.

I ran upstairs to my bedroom and opened my jewelry box. Under the secret compartment was an envelope with the other half of the rent. I heard the knock on the kitchen door, so I ran down and saw Connor standing there, wearing his usual jeans and a t-shirt.

I opened the door with a big smile on my face, hoping to fend off any anger he may be carrying for me being two weeks' late on the rent... again. "Connor! Hello, how are you? I bet you've come for the rent and I have it right here." I talked as fast as I could to keep him from giving me his usual speech.

He rubbed his white, balding head as his blue eyes softened. He was about my dad's age and was always very kind and forgiving. That's why it was so hard for me to be late on the rent. "I'm surprised you have the rent. I've only been looking for you for the past two weeks. Hannah, you're two weeks late."

"I know, I know and I'm sorry that I put you through this every month, but it's been a tough summer. Jobs are hard to come by for some reason." I handed him the envelope and smiled again. "Do you forgive me?"

His lips turned up into a smile as he slowly shook his head. "Of course I do, but as I've said every time I come for the rent, please don't be late again."

I walked out onto the deck carrying the rest of my sandwich and watched him get into his truck as I made my usual *promise* that I'd be on time next month. All the while knowing we'd be doing this same dance again. I shoved the last piece of bread into my mouth, went back into the house and swallowed the remains of my tea, and then headed out to find Melinda.

I drove down East Chapline Street and crossed over the Sharpsburg Pike and continued into town past the post office. Melinda lived in a historic stone house dating from the 1700s with a red brick barn at the back of the house, which contained her antique shop. I parked in the little pull-off parking area, grabbed the box, and headed toward the store.

Sharpsburg is a quaint historical town recognized for the Battle of Antietam, known to be the single bloodiest day in military history on 17 September 1862. I don't know much about the history, but the town roughly has a total of eight streets with alleys in between, lined up in a grid pattern with sidewalks made of concrete, brick, or stone.

I do remember reading that the town was founded in 1763 by Joseph Chapline and I think George Washington thought about putting the U.S. Capital between Sharpsburg and Shepherdstown, our neighboring town across the Potomac River. Most of the houses were here during the Civil War battle, some of which are grand, while others are simple but still very charming. We have a local gas station, post office, bank, pub, many churches, two bed and breakfasts, two guesthouses, restaurant and deli, and even a pharmacy. We've got it all.

I spotted the *Open* sign and entered through the door and looked toward the back, where Melinda stood chatting with a distinguished-looking gentleman with coal black hair and a finely trimmed moustache. Melinda was a sweet lady in her early sixties standing about five foot five with highlighted short blonde hair. She had lived in town about twenty-five years and knew all there was to know about antiques.

I saw her glance at me as her eyes danced and she gave me a smile. "Hannah, how are you? I haven't seen you around town lately. How's the photography business?"

"Oh, you know, a little slow." I walked past pieces of crockery, oil lamps, antique chairs and a pie safe. I reached Melinda and fell into her extended arms and gave her a hug. "I always love coming in here. It's been too long."

"Yes, it has." She turned toward the gentleman and said, "Hannah, this is my antiques partner and dear friend Harold Smay. Harold, this is a friend and neighbor, Hannah Mills. She lives just up the road. What brings you in today?"

I shook Harold's hand and set the box on an antique oak drop leaf table. As I opened the box and removed the tissue paper, I pulled out the blanket and handed it to Melinda and said, "This is what brings me here today. Do you know what type of Navaho blanket this is and if it's worth anything? It was left to me by my Great Aunt Dorothy, who died a few months ago."

I heard Melinda gasp as she leaned toward the window for more light and began to stroke the fabric in her hands. She then looked at Harold with wide eyes and asked, "Is this what I think it is?"

Harold then took the blanket in his hands and wore a poker face as the vein in his neck began to pulse. "I'm not sure, but I believe this is a Navaho First Phase Chief's blanket. There are only a few of them found in the country. Where did you get this again?"

"It was sent to me by my Great Aunt Dorothy's attorney from her estate. She passed away two months ago. Her letter stated that it might be worth something. She had seen something on the *Antique Road Show* that looked the same and was valued at almost a million dollars."

As Harold continued to inspect the blanket carefully, he then turned toward us and said, "I can have someone who has much more knowledge in this area than me appraise it for you, but I am almost positive this is genuine, and you may very well be correct in the value of this being close to a million, if not more."

I suddenly began to feel light-headed as Melinda grabbed hold of my arm and guided me to a chair. I couldn't believe what I just heard and felt the back of my neck tingle. I looked at Harold and said, "Does this person you know live in the area?"

"He works at Sotheby's in Haverford, Pennsylvania, outside of Philadelphia, but he travels quite frequently to my place in Hagerstown. I could have him here early next week. He's an expert in this area and would be able to authenticate it for you. I could set up an appointment. Is there any day or time that works better for you?"

I had a quick flash of my empty calendar and said, "Oh, I'm pretty open to any time, really. I can give you my cell phone number." I pulled out my business card and handed it to him as I steadied my hand.

Melinda smiled and gave me another hug and said, "You be sure to keep that locked up now, and we'll keep this between the three of us. It'd be best not to tell anyone. We wouldn't want anyone getting greedy."

I smiled and placed the blanket back into the box and left the shop and tried to catch my breath, knowing there was no way I could keep this a secret. I drove back to my place, ran upstairs and placed the box on the floor of my closet and then jumped back into my car, knowing full well I was headed to my brother's place to share the news with him and Mandy. After all, they were family; they knew how to keep a secret.

CHAPTER THREE

As I drove to meet Harold at his shop, I chuckled at the memory of Mandy and Justin's eyes when I told them I had a meeting to authenticate the Navaho blanket and that there was a strong possibility it was worth a lot of money. We all saw dollar signs, especially Justin, since I owe him roughly three thousand dollars. I was also surprised Harold was able to meet with me only a few days after we first spoke and I couldn't wait to get there. I hoped I wouldn't be disappointed.

I pulled into the Beaver Creek Crossroads Antiques parking lot off the National Pike and found a spot close to the entrance. I grabbed the box and walked through the alarmed doors and scared myself when I spotted an Indian Chief mannequin wearing sunglasses sitting on the hall bench. Who would do something like that? It was creepy.

I went through the second set of doors, and I saw Harold walking toward me with another gentleman who looked to be in his late sixties, wearing a crisp, white, short-sleeved button-down shirt with a flashy

1950s tie and tan khakis that were clearly too long, which caused his knees to bag.

He approached me and stuck out his hand and said, "You must be Hannah Mills. Harold has told me all about you and your blanket. My name is Jasper Collingsworth."

I shook his outstretched hand and noticed cataracts in his eyes and wondered how the hell he could authenticate anything with cataracts and who has a first name like Jasper? "Hello, it's nice to meet you."

They directed me past the main desk and back into a little room behind the register and we proceeded to discuss the story behind the blanket. I took it out of the box and laid it flat on the desk as directed by Jasper. I watched him caress the blanket, which was disturbing, and then he pulled out a magnifying glass and slowly gazed over the entire blanket.

After what felt like an eternity, he set the magnifying glass down and carefully lowered himself into a leather office chair. He again touched the blanket and said, "Miss Mills, I'm pleased to tell you that this blanket is indeed a genuine Navaho First Phase Chief's blanket. First Phase blankets are the earliest and rarest of the Navajo Chief's style. The smooth, shiny wool is hand-spun from the Churro sheep. Blue indigo dye from Mexico was used with natural white and brown-black wools. I can hardly believe my eyes. My heart is jumping a little fast right now."

I, too, needed to sit down and grabbed a stool from against the wall and plopped down before I blacked out. "So, what do you think it's worth?"

"Hard to say, that usually depends on what happens at auction, but I could see it going for at least a million." He stared at me with his black and white clouded, beady eyes and then looked over at Harold. "Was there any discussion regarding auctions or donations?"

Harold shook his head and then looked at me. "Hannah, have you given any thought as to what you would like to do?"

I was still numb from hearing the word 'million'. I tried to keep my knee from jumping and placed my hand on it to steady the nerves climbing up my leg. "I'm really not sure. Where would I take it for auction?"

Harold said, "I would be glad to do business with you at my auction house in Haverford, but only if you're comfortable with that prospect. I don't want to rush you into any decision."

"Okay, yes I think I'd like to take a few days to think about it, if that's okay with you? I want to be sure it's what Great Aunt Dorothy would have wanted."

"Absolutely, I completely understand. You have my card; give me a call when you've made a decision. In the meantime, you should be sure to place this in a safe place. I'd be glad to lock it here in our safe if that's what you wish."

I suddenly felt a chill down my neck and decided to keep the blanket close to me. It wasn't that I didn't trust Harold. He did business with Melinda. I just wasn't ready to let it go. "No, that's okay, I'll be sure to keep it safe."

They helped me wrap it up and place it back in the box as they followed me out to my car. I carried the box as if it were made of Tiffany glass. I waved goodbye and started to pull out of the parking lot when my cell phone rang. I looked at the name and quickly put the car into park and answered. "Hi, Mandy, what's up? You're never going to believe it. The blanket is worth... what, who is this?"

I heard a strange voice with an unfamiliar accent stop me short and tell me to listen carefully. My eyes began to water as I listened to the deep voice tell me that he had Mandy and that he was going to kill her if I didn't give him the blanket. He said he'd give me my instructions in an hour, but that I couldn't tell anyone, especially the police, or he'd kill her.

I shouted into the phone, "How do I know you have her? Let me talk to her!"

I heard a scuffle in the background, and then, as plain as day, Mandy's quivering voice came through and said, "It's true, Aunt Hannah. Do as they say, please."

The phone went dead, and I threw it on the dash as I leaned my head on the steering wheel and began to sob. *What just happened? Is this some sort of a joke? What am I going to do? How did they find out about the blanket? Jasper couldn't have told someone that fast.* I took a deep breath and wiped my eyes on my arm and then wiped my nose in my shirt. No time to worry about the stain.

I put the car back into reverse and started out again toward home. I needed to gather my thoughts and be sure I was ready for the next phone call in an hour. Who had Mandy? I couldn't quite make out the accent of the jackass who was talking on the other end. Was it French or Russian? I couldn't tell, but I'd be sure to listen carefully the next time I spoke to him.

My mind was reeling as I pulled into my driveway, grabbed the infamous box, and ran into the townhouse. Suddenly, the brightly painted walls felt dark and gloomy, and as I looked out the dining room window, my flowers weren't quite as brilliant as they were when I left to meet Harold.

It was to the minute when my phone rang again, and I snapped the phone off the table and put it on speaker. As I carefully listened to the instructions, I frantically wrote everything down on a piece of paper. My eyes grew wide as I yelled, "How in the hell am I going to get to France? I have no money."

The evil voice replied, "I don't care what you do. You book a room at the Hotel Regina in Paris in three days. If you don't, your niece is dead. Once you have arrived, you will call the number I gave you and wait for further instructions."

The phone went dead. I didn't even get a chance to speak to Mandy, although I knew she was alive because I could hear her yelling in the background, which made me sick to my stomach. I quickly grabbed my laptop and began to search for the Hotel Regina. I found the website and almost passed out as I read three hundred and five dollars a night. How was I going to get a plane ticket to France and pay for a room at this hotel? How many nights would I be there? All of my credit cards were maxed out, and I had no money. I couldn't ask Justin... hell, I couldn't tell anyone.

I got up from the dining chair and began to pace around my kitchen. *This can't be happening. I have to think straight. Who can I borrow money from? Who would have that kind of money?* I hurriedly ran upstairs and began to throw things into a suitcase. I grabbed the blanket and folded it neatly on top of my clothes and then sifted through my strongbox and pulled out my passport. It had two years left before it expired. The first and last time I traveled internationally was with Brett when we went to Ireland. Suddenly, my heart began to ache as I remembered that fabulous trip in the Emerald Isle.

I quickly shook my head and closed the suitcase. As I plopped down on the bed, I burst into tears and tried to think of a way to get my hands on a few thousand dollars. I needed something fast. I didn't have time to waste. Suddenly, an idea popped into my head and, before I could let the rational part of my brain stop me, I jumped up off the bed and began to search through my drawer. This was the only chance I had to save Mandy's life. Desperate times call for desperate measures.

———

My hands were shaking, and my upper lip was moist as I waited at the side of the building before closing. I watched Otto lock the bank vault and begin his routine of closing down for the day as I casually walked through the front door and immediately pulled a ski mask over my head and approached the counter.

My heart was beating faster than I could breathe as I gripped the toy water pistol in my pocket – I had found it in the yard, left by my neighbor's kid. I closed my eyes and took a deep breath and yelled to Otto in what I thought was a disguised voice.

"I'd like to make a withdrawal please."

What the hell kind of a bank robber says 'please'? I watched Otto turn around and stop short as he stared back at me. I wore a hoodie to cover my hair and gloves to disguise my hands. The sweat was dripping down my cleavage as I shoved the pistol further in my pocket and motioned toward the vault when I suddenly realized I should have emptied the water gun as I felt water run through the pocket and down my leg.

Otto slowly moved toward the counter and said in his weak, high-pitched voice, "Don't do anything rash. I'll get you want you need. Just don't shoot me."

He was the closing manager for the day, so nobody else was in the bank. I suspected the cameras were taping my every move, so I tried to walk in a hulk-like manner, which made me look even more ridiculous.

"I need two thousand seven hundred and eighty-two dollars. Get it for me now before I blow your head off." I was beginning to feel like Vin Diesel in *Fast and Furious* as I pumped up my chest and yelled, "Let's go! I don't have all day."

Otto suddenly stopped and turned around and whispered, "Hannah, is that you?"

I tried not to reveal myself while keeping my legs from going out from under me. "No and shut up, don't talk. Get me my money."

Otto ran to the desk and opened a drawer and pulled out some keys. He quickly opened another drawer from beneath the counter. He kept his head down and began to whisper, "What are you doing? Are you crazy? If you just needed some money, you could have asked me. Why are you doing this?"

I could feel the tears well up in my eyes and said, "Otto, I have to. I can't tell you why but this is a matter of life and death. I know this is being video-taped, but I didn't know what else to do. Whatever you do, please don't let anyone know that it's me. I beg of you, please. I'll turn myself in soon enough, but I have to do this."

I knew Otto had had a thing for me since high school. His face softened, and he gave me a light smile. "Why do you need such a specific amount?"

"Because that's what the plane ticket and hotel room cost."

"Plane ticket, hotel room? Where the hell are you going?" He quickly counted out the money and slid it under the glass window on the counter. "There's an even three thousand. I'll try to keep them from finding out as long as I can, but I can't promise anything."

I grabbed the money and before I could turn to leave, a woman in a mini-van pulled up to the drive-through window and screamed and began pointing in at me. I ran out the front door, and immediately pulled off the mask and then jumped into my car and pulled out onto Main Street. I turned onto Hall Street and then onto Chapline Street and raced up to my house. I pulled off my hoodie, threw the gloves on the seat and then ran into the house. I didn't have time to think, or realize that I had just held up my local bank!

I grabbed my suitcase, purse and passport and ran downstairs. I locked the door and jumped back into my car and made my way to the Baltimore airport. It would take me an hour and a half to get there, and I figured I could pay for my ticket for the next available plane to France with cash. I didn't want to leave any trace. Of course, that ship had probably sailed now that I committed a federal crime.

I arrived at BWI in better time than I thought and parked my car in long-term parking. I ran to the ticket counter at Air France and found the first ticket agent, a woman in her late fifties with a great smile and high-lighted auburn hair, and booked my flight. I couldn't stop my hands from shaking as I handed her the cash, showed my passport and driver's license, took my boarding pass and tried not to bite my lower lip off.

I only had a half hour before my flight boarded, so I quickly took my carry-on suitcase, which met the minimum size and headed toward security. This was always the irritating part of a trip. The line was short, so I began to remove my belt, my Fossil watch, and placed them in the plastic bin. Boy, was I glad I wasn't carrying any breast milk. I remember the woman who had to drink it herself to prove to TSA that it was real!

I made it through without setting off any alarms and quickly found the ladies room, evacuated my bladder, a strange term my grandmother always used, and ran to my gate. I had five minutes to spare as I heard the distinguished-sounding gentleman an-nounce that my flight was now boarding. I handed them my boarding pass, scurried along with the others like a herd of cattle, found my seat, threw my suitcase in the overhead bin, and plopped down into my seat. Thank goodness for aisle seats, because I needed the extra room from being pushed by the overweight lady next to me.

I didn't even have time to think what was taking place back at the Jefferson Security Bank after I was spotted wearing a ski mask. The whole scenario seemed surreal. Would I even make it to France, or would I find myself being hauled off this plane and taken into custody in handcuffs? I slowly leaned back in my seat and held my breath. When I saw the seat-belt sign light up and heard the engines begin to rumble, I blew out my breath and prayed I made it in time for Mandy. What would I tell Justin when he realized she hadn't come home? I'd figure that out when he called, but for now, I needed to focus on my plan, which was pretty sketchy at the moment, and save my niece.

———

I felt a tug on my shoulder, which ticked me off because I was in the middle of an amazing dream about Ryan Reynolds and he was just about to unhook my bra. The tugging wouldn't stop, so I opened my eyes and realized the woman next to me was letting me know we were about to land. Wow, I'd slept the entire flight!

Putting my seat back into the upright position, I rubbed my eyes. It was a straight seven-hour flight and when I glanced at my phone, the time had changed to eight fifteen in the morning, Paris time. I was doing great for my schedule and hoped I'd have an easy time arriving at the hotel. I had heard it was murder getting around in Paris.

I braced myself as the wheels touched down and I tried to pop my ears. I glanced out the window but could only see a fraction of the glass due to the giant side boob of my next-door neighbor blocking my view. I saw the seat belt sign go off and heard the instructions from the flight attendant as I hurriedly stood up and grabbed my suitcase out of the overhead compartment and tried not to lose my balance as I braced myself against the seat.

I rolled my eyes at the line of herded people bumping against each other as we exited the plane.

Flying economy seemed to bring out the beast in everyone, leaving no room for kind words or friendly smiles. You couldn't pay me enough to be a flight attendant. I broke free and took a deep breath of fresh air as I scurried past everyone in the Passenger Boarding Bridge, the name given by the handsome flight attendant, and walked toward the Customs gate. This line was shorter, which I was grateful for because I really needed to find the ladies room. As I approached the window, the burly woman with pudgy cheeks and tightly crimped blonde hair faintly smiled and asked for my passport. She then looked up at me and asked what my visit to France was for, and I kindly and smoothly replied, "For pleasure, madam."

She stamped my passport, handed it to me through the glass window opening, and wished me well. I shifted my roller suitcase to the other hand and swiftly found a brightly lit sign displaying a block-figured woman. I took care of my personal business, found the booth to exchange dollars to euro, and tried to find the terminal I was directed to earlier for the shuttle that would take me to the Hotel Regina. I immediately spotted the logo of the hotel and ran to catch the door before it closed.

The driver nodded and put the shuttle in drive before I had even found a seat. I sat down by myself and finally had the chance to catch my breath. It was just ten o'clock, and I read somewhere that it should only take about forty minutes to arrive in Paris center. I needed to take a shower desperately, but it would have to wait until I called for my instructions. I was relieved I didn't run into any police to be detained for what I had done at JSB. Maybe Otto was able to explain it away. or even replace the money before anyone found out. All I could do was hope I could pull this all off and get Mandy back home. I barely remembered the French I had learned in high school, and I only had enough money for a couple of days. I wasn't even sure how I would get Mandy back to the States.

I leaned my head back on the seat and closed my eyes. I didn't have time to worry about any of that now. I just needed to save Mandy. I didn't even care about the blanket. Her safety was all that mattered. I could feel my head roll to the side as I slowly felt my body relax. A few moments of rest would do me good.

CHAPTER FOUR

I FELT AN ABRUPT JERKING OF MY BODY AND MY head snapped forward as I realized the shuttle had come to a stop. The little boy in the seat ahead was laughing and pointing at me, and I immediately felt the saliva on my chin and wiped it with my sleeve. I scrunched up my nose and made a face and chuckled to myself when his mother told him to turn around. That'll teach him, I thought! The driver announced the arrival at the Hotel Regina in a few languages as people began to exit. I found an opening and followed suit and stepped out onto the sidewalk.

I gawked at the grand building made of faux marble, with tall windows encased with wrought iron balconies and the letters of the hotel name were made of gold. Well, I guess it wasn't actually gold, but then again, for the cost of a one night's stay, it may as well have been. I turned around to get a feel of where I was and my chin dropped. Off in the distance, directly across from the hotel, was the Eiffel Tower. I couldn't believe it! As many times as I've seen pictures and heard people describe what it felt like to see it for the first time, I was in complete awe and at a loss for words.

I caught myself and quickly turned and headed into the hotel. I wasn't here for sightseeing today. I entered the lobby, and the mesmerizing beauty continued as I tried to keep my chin from completely falling off. I couldn't keep my head from spinning around to see everything as I slowly made it to the front desk. The opulent woodwork, marble fireplace mantels, Persian rugs and golden embossed picture frames were just a few of the items I could take in with wide eyes.

The very sleek and refined woman at the front desk looked at me with her hazel eyes and smiled. I immediately began to tap my brain to see if I could remember what little French I had in high school and said, *"Bonjour. Je m'appelle Hannah Mills, parlez-vous anglais?"*

She smiled and revealed beautiful white teeth and said, *"Oui,* I do speak English. Do you have a reservation?"

"No, but I was hoping there was a room available. I have cash to pay." I fumbled in my purse and began to pull money out of the envelope when I heard her clear her throat. As I looked back at her, I realized I was making a fool of myself.

"No need for you to pay me now, Mademoiselle, you can pay when you leave. I only need a credit card to hold the room charges for you."

"I, unfortunately, don't have a credit card, but I do have cash."

She looked at me as if I had three heads and then looked at her computer screen. "That's not a problem, Mademoiselle. If you would like to pay a deposit for the first night's stay, that would be fine. I do have a room that faces the back of the hotel, if that is okay? Do you know how long you will be staying with us?"

"Oh yes, that's perfect, and no, I'm not sure how long I'll be staying. Can I let you know before the checkout time if I'll need another day?" I was glad the room was at the back of the hotel, the more out of the way, the better.

"*Oui.*" I watched her flawless French-manicured nails tap onto the keys of the computer as she stared at the screen. I thought it was an interesting concept for a Parisian to have a French manicure. She then swiped a card into a machine, placed it in a cardboard holder, and handed it to me. "Your room is one of our classic rooms on the fourth floor. You can get there by the elevators that are directly behind you. Enjoy your stay with us. If you need any assistance, you can call down to the front desk by punching in zero on your room phone."

I started to zone out listening to the sexy, light sound of her accent and caught myself staring at her. I sheepishly smiled and said, "*Merci beaucoup.*"

I grabbed my suitcase and trotted off to the elevator. I punched number four and leaned against the wall of the elevator and caught myself in the mirror. Wow, my hair was a mess. I had no idea I looked this bad. I hoped I could take a shower before I received my instructions, which suddenly reminded me again why I was here, as I tried to keep my emotions in check.

The elevator doors opened, and I walked down the hall to my room, slipped in the card, waited for the green light, and then entered through the door. The room was bright, with ivory painted walls, taupe sheers that draped to the floor, and a full-size bed with a taupe comforter. I set my suitcase against the wall and dropped face-first into the pillow, which felt like a cloud; not that I knew what a cloud felt like, but it was plush and soft. I had just started to drift off when I remembered I had to call the number I was given.

I wearily picked up my head and grabbed the phone. I dialed the number and slowly moved to a seated position and waited for someone to answer. It was a good thing I had added international calls to my plan before I left, but man, was I going to have a hell of a bill. The ringing stopped, and when I heard nobody on the other end, I said, "Hello?"

Then I heard the same strange voice give me instructions to meet in the park at the base of the Eiffel Tower in two hours' time. I was to come alone and put the blanket in a discreet bag from the hotel. He said I'd receive further instructions at that time. I quickly asked to speak to Mandy, after which I heard her cry to do as I was told, and then the phone went dead.

Tears welled up in my eyes and began to cascade down my cheeks. I couldn't tell if I was crying from exhaustion or the fear of not getting Mandy back... or both. Either way, I had to stop and clear my head. First things first – I needed a shower. Pulling my suitcase onto the bed and unzipping the lid, I quickly grabbed a change of clothes consisting of a white cotton, button-down oxford shirt, a clean pair of underwear and socks. I figured I could use the same bra and jeans I wore on the plane.

I stripped down, letting everything fall to the floor and ignored my mother's voice in my head to pick up the clothes and place them where they belonged. I jumped into the shower and blasted my face with hot water and immediately felt my muscles begin to ease. I grabbed the hotel shampoo and opened the lid and dumped the fragranced coconut-scented liquid on my head and lathered my scalp. I realized I could really enjoy this shower without having to worry about paying the water bill and decided to take the extra time to loofah my entire body. Why not? The loofah came with the room, and I was paying for it.

I dried off with the thick, plush cotton towel, got dressed, quickly did my makeup and blew my hair dry. As I started to brush my teeth, I felt my stomach begin to gurgle, and I realized I hadn't had anything to eat. I wasn't quite sure where to go, but remembered seeing a little café inside the hotel lobby that served croissants. I could grab something along the way and ask for a bag for my blanket.

Taking one last look in the mirror and ignoring the dark circles under my eyes, I grabbed my camera and threw it in my purse, and headed to the elevator. I arrived in the lobby and made my way to the café, only to begin an argument with the clerk in my broken French, to allow me to carry out my croissant and coffee. Apparently this was a real faux pas, but I had no time to waste, and I was starving. I graciously repeated "*Je suis désolée*" about a hundred times and ran out the door.

I made it to the street and was about to hail a taxi while shoving a piece of croissant in my mouth and trying to sip the hot coffee without spilling it on my shirt, when I felt someone grab my arm and pull me back. He spoke to me in what sounded like an Irish accent.

"Are you Hannah Mills?"

I swiftly whipped around, which caused me to

accidentally dump my coffee on a very tall and in-
credibly handsome brown-haired, green-eyed hunk of
a man's denim shirt. As I gazed up at him, I felt my
stomach flutter and my knees go weak. He was charis-
matic-looking, with a rugged two-day beard and
shoulders that looked like they could carry me away,
which is exactly what I hoped would happen... until
he pulled away and began to wipe his shirt and I saw
a formal identification card attached to his belt. I
froze. I realized this guy was either an FBI agent or
some other sort of an agent, and I had been caught for
robbing the bank. I could now do one of two things:
either I gave myself up and tell him what happened to
Mandy and run the risk of her being killed, or I could
jump in the taxi that had just pulled up while he was
distracted with the hot coffee that had apparently
scalded his chest. I chose the taxi.

Without thinking, I slammed the door shut and
screamed to the driver, "La Tour Eiffel, et dépêchez-
vous. There's a mad man after me!" I saw his eyes get
wide as he floored the gas and took off. I looked behind me and saw the handsome hunk slam his hand
on the back of the taxi and then take off at a run. I
gasped and then relaxed as I saw him stop in between
two cars, creating a small collision. I took a deep
breath and closed my eyes and then realized I had no
coffee to wash down the rest of my croissant with.

It took about fifteen minutes in traffic to arrive at
the Eiffel Tower, and I felt chills run down my spine
as its beauty came into full view. It was the most spec-
tacular work of cultural art I had ever seen. I immediately grabbed my camera and went into a shooting
frenzy.

The taxi stopped, and I handed him twenty euro,

which included a tip. He didn't seem to scoff at me, so I figured a three-dollar tip was sufficient. I thanked him and walked over toward the line of trees at the base of the iron monster. I couldn't take my eyes off the structure. My camera lens clicked off in a cycle of photos before I remembered what I had come here to do.

Putting the camera back in my purse and shifting the hotel bag containing the blanket in my right hand, I walked over to the trees and leaned against the park sign and waited for the next call, all the while looking in every direction, hoping the handsome agent wasn't around. But also wishing he was, because I couldn't seem to get that flutter out of my stomach.

I took a deep sigh and tried to shake off the jet lag that was beginning to take hold of me when my phone rang. I jumped and quickly answered to hear the next set of instructions, and then I remembered how high the roaming charges would be on my next bill. Oh well, I guess it didn't matter because I'd be going to jail, anyway.

I could hear Mandy screaming in the background as I gulped back my tears and tried to listen to the creep explain how to leave the hotel bag at the fifth tree directly behind me facing south. How the hell was I supposed to know where south was? I sucked at directions. I walked over to the fifth tree, took a guess where south was, dropped the bag, and walked toward the base of the tower as instructed. I wasn't supposed to wait around, but I had to have some way of spotting Mandy as he said he would leave her by the tree.

I tried to see a portion of the bag as I waited for someone to retrieve it and leave Mandy behind. It felt like forever before I noticed a black SUV pull to the side of where the taxi dropped me off, and a man with dark hair wearing a hoodie walk over to the bag. I looked left, and then right, and then back at the SUV waiting for Mandy to appear, but there was no sign of her. I started to panic as I watched him pick up the bag and look inside and then head back toward the vehicle.

I wasn't leaving there without Mandy, so I started to walk in a fast pace toward the SUV when, out of nowhere ,the gorgeous agent appeared right in front of me as I darted to my left and started to run toward the trees. I quickly leaned against one of the trees for cover and grabbed my camera and started taking pictures of the man jumping into the SUV and snapped off photos of the license plate. Before I could take cover, I felt the same firm grip on my elbow as I struggled and screamed to get away.

"Let go of me. You don't understand. They're getting away!" I shoved and pushed as hard as I could, and I felt him shove me up against one of the trees.

He looked straight into my eyes and spoke in an Irish lilted accent. "What the hell are you talking about? Who's getting away? Hannah Mills, I'm FBI agent Finn MacNally, and you are hereby under arrest for the bank robbery at the Jefferson Security Bank in Sharpsburg, Maryland."

There went my stomach again. What the hell was that all about? I stuck out my chin and glared into his stunning green eyes and said, "I don't care who you are. Those assholes in that black SUV over by the taxis just took my blanket without returning my niece."

He eased up on his grip and leaned back from my

face as he glanced over my shoulder toward the line of taxis. "I don't see any black SUV."

"No kidding, because they took off. I can't believe this is happening." I tried to shove him off my arm, but his grip only got tighter. "Look, I need to call them back, or try to see what happened. They were supposed to take the blanket and return my niece. It was supposed to be a trade."

"I don't know anything about a blanket or your niece, but I am here to arrest you for a bank robbery you committed in the States, and that's what I plan to do." He turned me around and shoved me against the tree as he placed handcuffs on my wrists.

"Ouch, that hurts! Why'd you have to tighten them so hard?" I felt him turn me back around to face him and I could feel my face getting hot as the tears started to fall down my face. I couldn't stop them. Then I could hear this ridiculous sound come from my throat and that's when all of the exhaustion and fear just exploded out of my mouth and mucous dripped down from my nose.

His face contorted into a pained look as he quickly grabbed my arm and started to pull me along the gravel walkway. "I think you need to tell me a little more about why you robbed the bank back in Sharpsburg and why you are now in France."

In between my sobs, my voice hitched, and I tried to explain what just took place in the park. After explaining everything and obviously receiving no sympathy, I remembered my camera and the photos I took of the SUV license plate.

"Wait a minute. I have pictures of the SUV. I can show them to you, and you can go after them. Isn't that what FBI agents do? Go after *real* criminals?

Speaking of which, you didn't show me your badge." I knew I had seen his ID, but I felt like irritating him since he didn't seem to care that my niece had been abducted.

He rolled his stereotypical Irish green eyes and flashed his badge in my face and returned it to his belt. He then proceeded to walk me to the side street and removed my purse from my shoulder and pulled out my camera. "Let's sit over here on the bench and take a look at the pictures you took."

I was beginning to enjoy having his hand on my upper arm as I tried to ignore my fluttering stomach again. Why did that keep happening? I shouldn't care how absolutely fine he looked and smelled. What was that scent? It was a clean, fresh fragrance. Okay, now my mind just went to the Irish Spring soap commercial. Man, why does my mind do that all of the time?

I sat down next to him and watched him try to figure out my camera. "You could just give it to me, and I could show you."

He gazed at me through narrow eyes and said, "Do you think I'm not capable of working it?"

"I think you're pretending you know what you're doing and we're wasting a lot of time."

I watched his lips tighten as he handed me the camera. "I'm starting to get cheesed off."

I don't know where it came from, and again it could have been my exhaustion, but laughter began to roll from my throat and out of my mouth as I leaned back on the bench. My eyes started to water, and I couldn't catch my breath. "What the hell does that mean? Cheesed off?"

I didn't hear any response, so I figured I'd better stop laughing and sit back up. I glanced over and caught his side grin. "Sorry, I've never heard that phrase before."

"It means you pissed me off."

"I sort of figured. Look, I can't show you the pictures on my camera with my hands in cuffs. Can you please remove them temporarily?"

I saw him wince and then my stomach dropped again, which clearly needed to stop happening. No matter what facial expression he made, he was ruggedly handsome. I watched him grab the key from his shirt pocket and unlock one of the cuffs from my right hand, and I felt the tight grip release from my wrist. "Thank you. Can I have my camera?"

He handed me the camera and said, "Here, I'm not sure what good this will do you, but I'll humor you for a bit."

I rolled my eyes and then proceeded to scroll through the last six pictures. I moved the screen toward him and began to roll through the images of the black SUV and license plate. "Here, this is the SUV, and that's the license plate. Oh, and this is a picture of the guy who took my blanket but failed to return my niece."

His eyes got wide, and then he asked, "Can you increase that image for me?"

I hit the zoom button and then handed him the camera. "There, you can see a very clear shot of his face while he looks back. Can't you do some kind of face recognition thingy and find him? He's kidnapped my niece for the ransom of my blanket. We had a deal. He didn't keep his promise."

He immediately tucked the camera under his arm and began to pull on my elbow to get up off the bench. "I think you'll need to come with me and meet another agent."

"Wait a minute, aren't you going to help me? You're going to blow me off just like that?"

I saw his jaw tighten and I decided to keep quiet. His eyes had a strange look to them; they were no longer the dreamy eyes I saw earlier. He carefully escorted me to his black Suzuki SUV and opened the back door. Inside were two men wearing jeans and button-down oxford shirts with blazers. Sheesh, I thought, do these guys actually coordinate their wardrobes before they leave for work?

"Hannah, these are agents Don Flook and Jim Flanders. Gentleman, this is Hannah Mills, and she has captured quite an interesting image on her camera." He flipped the camera screen toward them and showed them the image.

I watched their same reactions to the image, and it was killing me to know who this guy was. "Anyone going to fill me in on who he is?"

"I think you need to get in and have a chat with us about your niece." Finn opened the front door, and one of the cloned agents stepped out of the back and sat up front. He then guided me into the back next to the other twin and shut the door.

I looked in the rearview mirror at the brown eyes staring back at me, which apparently belonged to the driver and muscle of the group, because he looked to be about three hundred pounds and his arms were popping the seams of his matching oxford shirt. "So, which one of these guys is your superior?"

Finn smirked that ever-dashing smile and shook his head. "Neither of these men are. You'll meet one of the leading agents back at one of our safe houses."

"And where would that be, exactly? I have my things back at the hotel, and I need to use a restroom, if that's possible."

"We'll take you back to your room so you can get your things. You can use the restroom there."

"I paid cash for my room, which I shouldn't have to pay for a full day since I've only been checked in for three hours." I had hoped I could get a refund for the room. Maybe the classy woman at the front desk would give me a break, considering I was in handcuffs.

"We'll finalize everything with the hotel. Besides, the money you paid for the room isn't yours."

I suddenly felt my stomach roll again, but not for the same reason as before. "Oh yeah, well, there is that."

Finn looked at me with a side-glance and then looked out the window. "I have to ask you. What were you thinking when you decided to rob the bank? What went through your mind? Did you think you wouldn't get caught?"

My mouth went dry, and I couldn't seem to swallow. I suddenly realized the consequences were only beginning for me. I was going to jail. That's all there was to it. I would finally prove my mother right and be worth nothing in my life.

I tried to hold back my tears and said, "I wasn't thinking, that's the problem. I'm flat broke. I haven't held a real job for the last ten years. I've tried desperately to make it as a photographer but can't catch a break. Then I thought I had a chance with this antique blanket, and now this happened. So all I could *think* about was saving Mandy's life. Nothing else mattered. They told me not to go to the police or tell anyone. So I didn't and, since I had no money, I robbed the bank. I was going to pay the money back?"

He released an insulting chuckle and said, "You were going to pay the money back? What, like a loan? You held up the bank manager with a gun. Well, threatened him with what he thought was a gun. By the way, why didn't you empty the water pistol before you used it?"

"How did you know it was a water pistol?"

"We watched the surveillance camera footage. We saw where your pant leg got wet."

I saw smiles appear on all of the agents' faces as I slammed back against the seat. "I'm glad you all find this humorous. By the way, how did you find me?"

Finn replied, "We're the FBI. It's our job to find bank robbers. You left a trail that was easy to follow."

I chose to ignore his smug response and said, "Can we get back to the matter at hand and discuss who it is that has my niece? It's pretty obvious from the looks on your faces that you know who it is in that picture."

Finn's smirk disappeared, and he looked straight at me, and I could feel the heat shoot up my neck and then to areas that made me uncomfortable in my seat. "We need to discuss that in detail when we get back to our safe house. In the meantime, let's get your things."

CHAPTER FIVE

THE SUV STOPPED IN FRONT OF THE HOTEL AND Finn jumped out of the car and again grabbed my elbow and pulled me out of the seat. He casually moved to my left side and yanked on the one handcuff still attached to my left wrist. "You need to keep yourself in check and not try anything stupid."

"As if everything I've done to this point wasn't stupid?" I didn't get a response, so I tried to keep in stride with his long, muscular legs as we entered the hotel. I felt that tingle again. Wow, it was pretty obvious it had been a long time since I'd had any sex. That thought depressed me, because it had been six months since I last had sex. Okay, now I was lying to myself, because it was more like a year!

I realized agent Finn was staring blankly at me with his gorgeous green eyes as I drifted back to us standing in the elevator. He had apparently said something to me, and I had no clue what it was. "Did you say something?"

"Aye, I did. What floor are you on?"

"Oh, sorry, my mind drifted off a bit. I must be hungry. I'm on the fourth floor in room – oh shit! I can't remember what room I'm in. The key holder is in my purse, and so are the keycards, which are in the SUV."

I watched his cheeks puff out like a blowfish as he caught the elevator door before it closed. "Come on, let's get your purse."

After a bit of chaotic back and forth to get the keycards, we finally made it up to my room to get my belongings. Finn removed the cuff, and I decided to use the bathroom. When I looked in the mirror, I almost screamed. My mascara had washed off my lashes after my crying jag and was splattered under my eyes. I looked like I had risen from the dead.

I quickly washed and dried my face, which left foundation residue on the towel. No big deal, I wasn't paying for the room. I pulled the makeup bag out of my purse and swiftly did a makeover, which helped me look more human, but had me wondering why I cared. With the predicament I was in, not only was I never going to have sex again, it certainly wasn't going to be with agent dreamboat. Who knew how many years I'd serve in jail?

I took a deep breath and opened the bathroom door and saw three men standing in stereotypical FBI stances, looking back at me with that *she's finally out of the bathroom* look. Why do men always make women feel like they take up too much time in the bathroom? "What! I needed to freshen up, is that okay?"

Finn looked at his watch and said, "We need to get a move on if we plan on finding your niece."

"You're actually going to help me find my niece? You're not just saying that, are you?"

His face suddenly changed from being stern and

official to compassionate and sexy. "I just spoke with my superior after I sent him the picture you took. Actually, one of the IT guys sent the picture. Anyway, he's allowed me to fill you in on a case we've been working on for the last year and a half, which could affect the outcome of your niece's future."

I slowly sat down on the chair next to the bed and tried to keep my stomach from rolling, which was a completely different feeling from before. "What do you mean, affect Mandy's future?"

He averted his eyes and quickly walked over to the window and stared out toward the Eiffel Tower. "Ms Mills..."

"Whoa, that can't be good, you're calling me Ms."

He continued to keep his back toward me and said, "The gentleman, and I use that word loosely, that you captured in the photo works for a man named Borya Ivankov. He is a Russian drug lord who has recently tapped into the vile, but very profitable, world of human trafficking. He has traveled to the States and back with his drug runners and has committed enough crimes to have landed him in jail for three lifetimes."

"Why haven't you been able to catch him?"

He slowly turned around and then leaned against the window, causing the curtain to shade his face. "Because he's smart and has more money than God and can pay people off to keep him from getting caught."

"So you think he has taken Mandy for human trafficking? What does that mean, exactly? Is he selling her into prostitution?" I couldn't keep the tears from falling down over my cheeks. My face got hot, and I could feel the room spin around me as I tried to prevent myself from passing out.

He glided from the window and immediately sat on the bed and grabbed my arm. "Ms Mills, you don't need to think about any of that right now. What you need to focus on is helping us find her and possibly catching Ivankov. This is the first solid lead we've had in nine months. We actually have a license plate to go on now."

I walked over to the nightstand and grabbed a tissue from the box and blew my nose. I didn't care that I sounded like a foghorn. My life had completely turned upside down over a stupid blanket. "I don't know how I'm able to help."

"You've had contact with them. We need you to keep that line of communication open."

I looked at him as if he was completely nuts. "In case you haven't noticed, they didn't return Mandy to me. They took the blanket. I guess I don't have a whole lot of influence on these assholes."

The corners of his mouth turned up slightly as he stood up, from the bed and faced me. "You have fire in your belly, which is a good start. You're gonna have to trust me. Can you do that?"

For the first time, I really looked up into his eyes as the hair on the back of my neck stood up and all of my female urges began to erupt. I tried to keep my composure and said, "Yes. Yes, I do."

"Good, then let's get your belongings and head over to one of our safe houses. There's quite a bit of information we need to share about Ivankov, and we'll need to set up a meeting point." He glanced down at me from his six-foot-five frame and then opened the door. "You're still under arrest, so you need to re-member to keep yourself in check."

"I think I'm too hungry to try anything. Do you think I could get something to eat?"

"Aye, we'll get you something back at the safe house."

———

Within ten minutes, we arrived at an amazing historic building made of limestone with a tall, walnut wooden door. One of the other agents got out first and punched the keypad on the side of the building and then pushed open the door. Another guy, who I as-sumed was also an agent, poked his head out and nodded at Finn.

I followed their lead and got out of the SUV and im-mediately took in the beauty of the neighborhood. The buildings were like skyscrapers, barely allowing enough sunlight to shine on my face. I took a deep breath and smelled the aroma of coffee and pancake batter. My stomach did another dive, and I thought I would faint.

Finn grabbed my elbow and said, "Are you okay?"

"What is that amazing smell?"

"Aye, that would be the infamous smell of crêpes on a griddle."

"That's what I want. I'd love to try that."

"I'll send one of the agents to bring some back. You'll be glad you tried them."

"What are they?"

He smiled that devilish smile and kissed his fin-gers into the air. "As the French would say, they are *magnifique*. They are like a very thin pancake made of wheat or buckwheat batter, poured onto a flat, circular hotplate. They can be filled with anything you like, or you can eat them plain. Personally, I like them topped with whipped cream or powdered sugar."

As I followed him into the building, I thought I caught saliva sitting on my lower lip. I swallowed hard and tried to ignore my hunger pangs and then tried to adjust my eyes to the dark, small foyer. We entered through another door and found ourselves in front of a two-person elevator.

"How old is this building?"

"I believe it's dated to the nineteenth century."

He pushed the button, which unfolded a tiny glass door, allowing me to enter first at the back. He stepped in and barely missed hitting his head on the ceiling of the elevator. I could feel his warm arm against my shoulder as I forgot about my hunger and remembered that I hadn't had sex in a very long time. He hit the number four as the door closed, and we began to glide up.

We stopped, and he pushed the door open, and I followed him out into another tiny, circular foyer facing three doors. He pulled out a very large skeleton key and slipped it into the middle door. It unlocked as he stood out of the way for me to enter first. Wow, he was chivalrous, too!

The hardwood floors creaked beneath my feet as I entered an apartment of modern features nestled in a historic building. We were immediately standing in a small, rectangular foyer with open shelving on the right holding dishes, glasses, and silverware. The tiny kitchen on the left consisted of stainless steel appliances, butcher-block countertops, and a black and white speckled ceramic-tiled floor.

The toilet was separate from the bathroom, which was a common thing in France, and the one bedroom and living area had the typical ceiling-to-floor windows with wrought iron balconies. There were agents strewn around the living room, sitting in chairs, wearing headphones and staring at computer screens. They casually looked up at me and then returned their gazes to their work.

My stomach let out a noise that caught Finn's attention as he spoke in French to another agent and pointed out the window. I had no idea he could speak French, but then again, I didn't know anything about him. The agent smiled and stood up from his computer, removed the headphones, and made his way out the door.

"I told him to bring back some crêpes. I think we could all do with something to eat." Finn guided me over to a man in his fifties who balancing on the back two legs of his chair and wearing a Bruce Springsteen t-shirt and scruffy jeans. His hair was amber and cut tight to his head, and his eyes were as blue as the delphiniums in my garden. "Hannah, this is agent Tom Sliwa. He's been following Ivankov for the past three years. He knows every intricate detail of Ivankov and is all a-tingle that you caught one of his men on your camera, as well as a license plate number."

I met his extended hand and said, "Hello, nice to meet you... I think."

He smiled and exposed his blinding white teeth and pointed to his laptop screen, which displayed the images I caught magnified at least fifty percent. "This is a huge lead for us. We can finally run a trace on the plate."

Recognizing he was American, I somehow felt a

little more relaxed, in a strange sort of way. "I'm glad my images can help."

Finn asked, "Were you able to come up with anything?"

He nodded his head and said, "We were able to trace it to a car dealership up in Arras, which is where we had previous leads that Ivankov had a hideout in the small village of Rivière, just outside of Arras."

I zoned out of their conversation and casually looked around the small living area with its wooden pine floors and plastered walls. The ceiling had one of those intricate plaster medallions that encircled an empty space where a possible chandelier had hung. There wasn't any furniture except a few desks and chairs for the agents and two tall floor lamps. The curtains, a dark burnt orange, were drawn shut, making the room very dark and depressing.

I heard the door open, and instantly smelled the aroma of pancakes and I felt my stomach bind in hunger. I turned and saw one of the younger agents carrying three white take-out bags with grease stains on the corners. He set them on one of the desks and tore open the ends.

Without thinking, I grabbed one of the foil plates and lifted its lid and delicately snatched a crêpe covered in powdered sugar, rolled it like a jelly roll, and shoved half of it into my mouth. The taste was indescribable.

"You've got powdered sugar on your face." Finn handed me a napkin and shook his head. "What do you think?"

I finished chewing the amazing fried dough and smiled. "I've never tasted anything like this. It's fantastic, and that isn't just because I'm starving."

Finn smiled and took a bite of a lighter colored crêpe and said, "You're eating a crêpe made with the buckwheat flour. This one here is made with white flour."

"I eat buckwheat muffins all of the time, but this has a sweeter taste to it." I finished shoving the last piece in my mouth and already planned on eating one made with white flour topped with strawberries.

Tom handed us each a cup that looked as tiny as my childhood tea set. "Here's some coffee to wash down the crêpes. When we've finished, we can continue discussing our next steps to set up a meeting between you and Ivankov's men."

I choked on the coffee because it tasted horrible and I couldn't believe what he just said. "What do you mean, *me* meeting with one of Ivankov's men, and what kind of coffee is this?"

Finn chuckled and grabbed the cup from me and set it on the table. "That was espresso, and you might do better with water. You know we discussed earlier that we had an in now, for you to stay in contact with Ivankov's crew. We reached out to them from your phone and sent a text. They'll be contacting you very soon. They won't be able to resist."

I grabbed a bottle of water and chugged it down, allowing the dough to slide down my throat and then sat down in an empty chair. "What makes you so sure they can't resist?"

Finn picked up my phone from the makeshift desk of one of the agents, removed the charger cable, and showed me the text they had sent. I slowly read the words, *Did you honestly think that blanket was authentic?* "What makes you think they'll believe me?

They've probably found someone to authenticate it already. When did you get my phone?"

"No, they wouldn't have had time yet. Don't worry. We'll hear something soon. And when they do, we'll have something to bargain with, which is a good thing for your niece, no?" Tom casually snatched the phone from Finn and placed the cable back in its end. "One of the agents brought your phone here before you arrived."

I glared at Finn, wondering when that exchange took place. Now that my stomach was content after eating three crêpes and sloshing down a bottle of water, I started to feel queasy from the thought of dealing with these assholes again. It was true. It did give us some leverage to find Mandy. My only hope was that she was still with them and hadn't been sold off to some prostitution ring.

"So if they do contact me, what's the plan then? Are we going to just sit around and wait for them to return my text? Mandy could be halfway around the world by then."

"No, we're going to follow our lead on the plate registered in Arras. You're going to come with us in case they do reach out to us. It's possible they still have your niece with them there." Tom glanced at Finn and then walked over to his laptop and sat back down.

I rolled my eyes and said, "He's real friendly. You know he could stop calling her my niece and call her by her name. She is a human being."

Finn slid a chair next to me and sat down. "They've been tracking Ivankov for a long time. They don't want to lose any leads, and unfortunately, your niece isn't a real priority for them. She's just a bargaining chip, and you should consider yourself lucky to be involved to this point. I was supposed to have you on a plane back to America two hours ago."

I could feel the heat rise up my neck and slowly reach my cheeks as I tried to keep the tears from spilling again. "Bargaining chip? Mandy's a bargaining chip? I'm supposed to feel lucky? I get what I did was clearly a federal offense, but my hands were tied. Her life was threatened, and I wasn't allowed to tell *anyone*. Do you understand how frightened I was? I had no other options, and I had *no* money. How the hell was I supposed to fly here in the timeframe they gave me? My parents and brother are going to be worried sick. By now, they haven't heard from Mandy and are wondering where I am."

Finn grabbed my hand, and it caught me off guard. I felt a surge shoot up my arm and I heard my heart beating in my ears. He softly smiled and said, "It's getting late, and I think you could do with some sleep. We won't be going to Arras until the morning. Why don't you go into the bedroom and get some rest? You've been up almost twenty-four hours."

I couldn't deny I was exhausted. My head was pounding, and my ears were ringing. I slowly stood up and said, "Yeah, I need some sleep. My head's in a complete fog. Where's the bedroom?"

"It's next to this room on the left. I'll tell everyone to keep it down." He stood up and walked me out of the living area and pointed to the left.

I nodded my head and entered the room and then shut the door behind me. The room was empty except for the bed and another tall lamp in the corner. The navy curtains were already drawn shut so I slipped off my shoes, plopped down onto the mattress, and then pulled the covers up to my chin. The bed was a bit lumpy, but I didn't care. At this point, I'd have slept on the floor. As I tried to quiet my mind and keep myself from crying for Mandy, I felt my body become limp. I took a deep breath and slowly allowed myself to float off into the dark abyss.

CHAPTER SIX

I FELT MYSELF SHAKING AND ROLLING AS IF I HAD fallen off a cliff. My eyes were pasted shut, and I could hear a voice in my ear. As I tried to squeeze my pillow, I realized someone was shaking my shoulder. I slowly pushed my eyes open and saw the handsome, blurry Finn kneeling next to me. I dreamily smiled and then noticed the firm look on his face and remembered where I was and that he wasn't waking me for a romantic tryst.

"Is it morning already?"

"Aye, early morning. We received a text message back from one of Ivankov's men. They took the bait. And it looks like the plate matches what agent Sliwa stated about Ivankov having a safe house in Rivière. They want to meet you. They're going to call in an hour with instructions."

I sat up and tried to stretch my shoulders and back and felt my stiff muscles ache as a result of the lumpy mattress. "What time is it?"

"It's half past four. You need to get yourself together, so you're alert and ready for the phone call. If you need to freshen up, we've placed your bags in the bathroom. There's some fresh coffee and croissants on the counter in the kitchen."

"Geez, I'm not a morning person, just so you know." I pulled the covers off and rolled over until my feet hit the floor. I rubbed my eyes and felt the gritty muck roll onto my fingers. I knew I looked frightful so I tried to remain casual as I stood up and walked out of the room and into the kitchen.

The apartment was all-abuzz with sounds of laptop keys chattering away and the hum of voices coming from the living area. I smelled the coffee as my head and stomach cried out for a wakeup call, but I scurried into the bathroom first to take care of more important things, like relieving my full bladder and washing my face. I refused to look in the mirror because it would only depress me, so I ignored myself and ran my fingers through my hair and brushed my teeth. Which was a dumb thing to do since I was about to have coffee and a croissant, but I didn't need to be barbaric and let anyone smell my morning breath.

I slipped out of the bathroom and into the kitchen to find the coffee. There was a French press sitting on the butcher block counter with cups, spoons, sugar, and creamer placed around the glass pot. There were remnants of spilled coffee strewn all over the counter, which made me aware I was in a room filled with men who didn't clean up after themselves.

Luckily, I found a clean cup and poured my cream in first, followed by the coffee. It smelled amazing. I stirred the cream until it turned to the toffee color I prefer, took a sip, and then grabbed a croissant and headed into the living room.

Finn turned toward me and nodded and then

picked up my cell phone and walked toward me. "Hang onto this. They'll be calling in about forty minutes."

I took a bite of the croissant and closed my eyes. I could taste chocolate. Whoever decided to place chocolate in the center of a croissant should be given a gold medal because my taste buds were in heaven. When I opened my eyes, Finn was staring at me. "Why are you staring at me? Haven't you ever seen someone eat a croissant filled with chocolate for the first time?"

He gave me that familiar smirk and said, "I think your eyes rolled back into your head. Why don't you have a seat over there and finish your *decadent* croissant, while we discuss what we want you to say when they call you?"

I walked over to the closest chair and sat down. I set my coffee on the edge of a desk and took another bite of bliss. As I washed down the remains of the puffed pastry with my coffee, I glanced at Finn and asked, "What am I supposed to say to them when they call?"

"We're not sure if they'll ask you about the blanket, but if they do, just tell them you grabbed one from the lobby of the hotel."

I started to giggle and said, "Seriously, you think they're going to believe that? Look, that blanket doesn't look like an average throw blanket. They're bound to know I'm lying."

"That's why we're going to have you sweeten the pot and tell them that you also have a rare pink diamond ring that was given to you by a business partner."

"And where the hell am I supposed to come up with that?"

Finn walked over to agent Sliwa's desk and grabbed a gray felt pouch. He came back over to me and set it on my lap. "Take a look."

I opened the pouch and poked my thumb and finger inside until I felt a ring. I pulled it out and gawked at the pink stone glistening back at me. "Is this real?"

"Yes, it is."

"So, why is it you would use a real pink diamond for this exchange and not think they know the blanket they have *is* real?"

"One of Ivankov's businesses is diamonds. He'll have someone there that can authenticate it. And, if they have authenticated the blanket and know you're lying, this diamond will be too much for them to pass on."

"Do you want to explain to me how Mandy fits into the equation?"

"You'll make it clear that you want her in exchange this time, or you're going to go to the police. You'll demand no screw-ups this time."

"And you think that's enough? That they'll be willing to exchange her for the authentic blanket and a pink diamond ring? Who's to say Ivankov doesn't have enough money and diamonds even to care what I have in exchange?"

"Because you're going to tell him you have a contact in the States that can get him a very large shipment of rare diamonds."

I stared at him as if he had three heads. "I'm going to *what*?"

"You'll need to get familiar with a script that

should lure Ivankov to do business with you. We've included some names of people that we know are in the diamond business. It'll also explain how you came to have the blanket. That your family deals in *rare* antiquities. Don't worry. We know all of Ivankov's moves. He'll go for this."

"And if he doesn't?"

"Come on, Ms Mills, don't be so pessimistic."

"I'm not pessimistic. I'm a realist, and I've never been involved in anything like this or dealt with anyone such as Ivankov. The only thing I care about is getting Mandy back. So I'm going to put my trust in you, but I swear, if this all goes to hell and she ends up in some prostitution ring, I promise I'll hunt you down. I don't care how long it takes or how long I'm in jail. I'll hunt you down."

"And do what?"

"Don't worry. I'll have a long time to figure that out. And if it lands me back in jail for the rest of my life, it'll be worth it."

His expression revealed he understood my candor. He carefully took the ring from me and placed it back in the pouch. "You'll need to get ready for their call. You have about ten minutes."

I held my phone and nervously waited for *the* call and carefully read their script. What a strange place I found myself to be in, reading a script written by a bunch of FBI agents coaching me what to say to a drug and human trafficking asshole.

I put the paper on my lap and pulled up the photos from my iPhone. The very first image was a selfie of Mandy and me crossing our eyes and sticking out our tongues. It was taken at her graduation. I'd have given anything to be back at that very moment, laughing and eating dinner at the Old South Mountain Inn. My brother arranged everything to the highest standard for Mandy's graduation. I knew he had to be worried sick. If I could only call him and let him know where I was, but I needed to wait until I had Mandy with me on the plane... along with an FBI agent and me in handcuffs.

Before I could wallow in that scenario, my phone rang, and I froze in mid-stare at Mandy's name on my screen. At once, four agents were surrounding me with discerning looks on their faces, but the only eyes that met mine were Finn's. He nodded his head, and I hit the accept button and put the phone to my ear and waited for my instructions with the ready-made script in my other hand.

I knew the agents were tracking the conversation and documenting the information. I calmly said hello and remembered the voice I had dealt with in earlier dialogues, which caused my skin to crawl, as I tried to concentrate on the script. The voice began to tell me that I would receive another call in two hours and that I had to travel to the E-Leclerc supermarket in the village of Arras and wait in the parking lot. They wanted to be sure I wasn't being followed or had anyone with me. The phone disconnected and one of the younger agents took the phone from me and hooked it up to a laptop.

I turned my gaze toward the window and saw the sun peeking through the clouds. I thought how strange to be in France and not have the chance to enjoy it. I saw Finn approach me out of the corner of my eye as I continued to stare at the grey zinc rooftops. "So, how do I find this supermarket?"

"You're going to be wearing one of these in your

ear, and we'll give you directions. We'll program the GPS."

I glanced over and saw what looked like the tip of a pinky. It was beige with a teeny-tiny wire at the end. "Where does this go?"

"In your ear and we'll be on the other end so we can communicate with each other. I'll be following you from a distance. You did a fine job of remembering the script. I think you sold them on the diamonds."

Finn shuffled his feet as he stood over me. I turned and looked up into his emerald eyes and thought his face looked softer somehow. "I guess we'd better get going then. So tell me, what happens at the next checkpoint? What if they keep jerking me around?"

"They may have you go to a few more checkpoints, but they're interested in dealing diamonds with you. Ivankov is a businessman who likes to make money any chance he can. Come on. We need to get you settled in a nondescript vehicle. It takes a little more than an hour to make it to Arras. We'd better get a move on."

I let out a big sigh and stood up. I felt defeated. I also looked like a dwarf standing next to Finn. In fact, he towered over everyone in the room. Not to mention his shoulders were broader and you could see his firm abs through the tight gray Henley shirt he wore. Okay, there it went again, all those tingling feelings in my abdomen and other places.

I shook off the yearnings and went into the bathroom to brush my teeth and put on my makeup. I could have used another shower, but there wasn't any time. I spotted my suitcase in the corner next to the shower and remembered I threw in my beige Antietam baseball cap. My safety net when I was having a bad hair day, which was now.

My skinny jeans looked like they had another day's life left in them. My black biker ankle boots were comfortable enough. I decided to do a PTA bath, which was another term my Great Aunt had shared with me that meant washing the essential parts of my body. I smiled at the memory and then felt awful that I wasn't fulfilling her wish for me to do right by the blanket. I guess in a way, I was. I was using it to save Mandy's life. Now I was thinking about Mandy and getting depressed again.

I had to quit thinking and finish getting ready. I put on my deodorant, my makeup, and then grabbed a clean chambray button-down shirt and tucked the front tails into my jeans. I combed my hair back and slipped on the hat and took one last glance in the mirror. I looked pretty good.

I tucked my makeup bag into my suitcase and zipped it shut. I grabbed the handle and opened the bathroom door only to find three agents leaning against the wall staring at me. Why do they do that? I glared back, giving them my usual 'get the hell out of my way' look. You'd think they'd take a hint.

I spotted Finn by the window looking over at me, wearing his sexy smirk. He obviously liked the hat. That boosted my confidence so I thought I'd give him a sexy look back, which caught the attention of the other agents and we all awkwardly looked down at the floor.

Finn walked toward me holding a folded map and said, "Now would be a good time to put your ear bud in. Nice hat, by the way."

I slipped the tiny finger in my right ear and adjusted it to a comfortable position. "Thanks. It's a necessary clothing staple for bad hair days. Are we ready to go?"

"I believe we are. The car is parked out front. It's already been programmed to our destination, but I've got a map to be sure we're on the right track. Can you drive a standard?"

I could feel my eyes get big and I knew I looked like a deer in headlights as I tried to casually relax my face and said, "Sure, I think I can remember how to drive a stick, but it's been a while."

I was using terms my father used when he tried to teach me to drive his rusted-out tan 1990 Ford Taurus Mercury Sable. It took me back to the memory of my body being thrown into convulsions trying to get the car to move five feet. I could never get the hang of the clutch.

Finn's eyebrows went up. "It can get tricky driving around the streets of Paris. Do you think you can handle it?"

"Of course I can handle it." Wow, I'm really going to hell for all the lies I've been telling!

"It'll be easier on a straight highway. Besides, the Alpha Romeo is a six speed, so it'll be a smooth ride. They'll more than likely ping your cell phone location, which is why we have a program to pick up on anyone tracking your locale. We may get lucky and find Ivankov's safe house."

I grabbed my camera, purse, and suitcase and followed Finn out into the hall and back into the elevator. This time I was in front, while he stooped and stood in the back. We reached the ground floor and headed out into the street, where a slick black Alpha

Romeo SUV was parked with its flashers blinking. One of the older agents, who looked about my dad's age, nodded at me and opened the door on the driver's side. I turned to look at Finn, but he was already getting into one of the black SUVs they were driving earlier. I smiled at the kind agent who put my suitcase in the back.

Shaking my head, I let out a big sigh, and slid into the driver's seat. "What do I do now?"

I heard Finn's voice in my ear. "As soon as you are ready, hit the GPS button."

I set my camera and purse on the front passenger seat and buckled my seatbelt, then flashed back to the age of sixteen to remember my dad's words of encouragement and instruction. I pressed the clutch, put it in neutral, started the engine, removed my foot for a second and hit the clutch again, shifted to first gear and heard the engine rev. Before I could move my foot from the clutch to the gas pedal, the car shook like a tilt-a-whirl ride at a carnival. The car leaped forward and stalled and stopped.

I again heard his voice say, "Are you having a wee bit of trouble?"

"Sorry, I told you it'd been a while since I've driven a standard. Don't worry. I'll get the hang of it, just give me a few more minutes."

I could feel the sweat drip down my back as I tried the whole process over again and carefully moved my foot from the clutch to the gas pedal. This time, the car was less violent and began to roll forward. I looked to my left and gradually pulled out onto the street and shifted to second. I heard the automated voice begin giving directions in French.

"Okay, this isn't going to work. I speak a little

French, but I'll never be able to follow these directions."

I'd started pushing buttons when, out of nowhere, a taxi driver pulled out, and almost sideswiped me. I jerked the steering wheel and swerved to the left and then back again. My heart was pounding in my throat. Before I could get acclimatized, I heard the engine whirl, and I realized I needed to change gears again.

Again, the voice in my ear said, "Do you think you'll make it out of the city?"

"Look, I'm going to take this earpiece out if you don't stop wise-cracking. I was trying to switch the GPS to English. I think I finally have it figured, so yes, I'll make it out of the city."

I heard a low chuckle, and I slammed on the gas pedal to keep up with traffic and began to make my way toward the A1. "So, agent McNally, are you married?" Why the hell did I start the conversation with that question? I'm such an idiot, especially now that there's an embarrassing silence.

"No, I'm not. I haven't found the time or met the right woman."

My mouth was dry, and I tried not to swallow my tongue. "I can imagine it would be difficult. I dated a guy for a while and thought we'd get married, until he cheated on me and left me in the middle of the night." Oh boy, I'm really painting a great picture of myself.

"Sorry to hear that. We're almost at our exit, so you need to pay attention to the road signs."

I could tell he was trying to change the subject, which was fine by me. Before I knew it, I was on the A1 and gaining speed as I continued to shift into higher gear and move along with the flow of traffic. I looked in the rearview mirror and could see Finn three cars behind.

I smiled and continued to run the driving steps through my mind and said, "See, I told you I'd get the hang of it."

CHAPTER SEVEN

Finn asked, "How long has it been since you've driven a standard?"

"I have to be honest, I've never really driven a standard. My dad taught me in his car when I was learning to drive, but then eventually he got an automatic and that was that."

"I see. Well, you seem to have a grasp of it now. We're tracking your phone, so if they are trying to ping it, it'll have you in their sights."

"Do you really think they're going to meet with me for this pink diamond, and will they exchange it for Mandy this time?"

I could hear him take a breath and say, "I do believe they'll meet with you. As far as the exchange is concerned, I'm not sure."

That wasn't what I wanted to hear. "Are you able to tell me what kind of a man Ivankov is? I know things are top secret, but I think I should know the reality of Mandy's situation. I've heard of human trafficking, but to be honest, I don't know what that involves."

"There are different ways of human trafficking.

One way is to set up an administrator in a foreign country outside of Russia, who sets up an apartment and obtains a phone number and begins advertising jobs in the newspaper for hospitality positions, or strippers. It would normally offer high pay, no experience required, and travel around the world, which entices women from rural countries. Another administrator at another business site then interviews these women. What they look for is women who have very little education, are desperate to leave their current situation, and have minimal family ties in Russia that would cause family members to search for them."

"What's the other way?"

I heard him clear his throat as he said, "Another way is to set up a bus tour through a new travel agency, offering a one-time-only discounted trip to visit cities such as Prague, or other Eastern European cities that don't require a visa for Russian citizens. The women are screened the same way and when they arrive, their passports and documents are taken from them, and they're forced into prostitution, striptease clubs, or massage parlors."

I tried to keep my eyes from watering and blinding me as I stared at the highway in front of me. The cars whizzed by, and I felt my head start to pound. I wasn't sure if I wanted to hear any more, but I had to know what I was getting into.

I quickly wiped the tears from my cheeks and asked, "Do you even think Mandy is still alive?"

"I do, actually. I think they have plans for using her in one of their criminal acts, but I also think they haven't had time to move her. I think we have a good chance of finding her, but I also want you to be prepared for the worst."

I dreaded hearing those words but had thought the same thing myself. "I know, I'm not naive, but I'm hopeful. I'm not leaving France until I have Mandy with me, so I'll do whatever it takes. I'm counting on you."

We didn't talk any further after that last statement. It was almost a silent affirmation between the two of us. We continued the drive in silence, which wasn't an easy thing for me. After forty minutes or so, I couldn't take the silence any longer and decided to look for a rest stop. My nerves had me needing a pee break.

"Do you think we could make a pit stop? I need to use the facilities."

"Look for a sign that shows a tree representing a picnic area. It'll be more private and easier to park out of the way of other vehicles."

I began to watch the road signs and came across one showing precisely what he stated, turned on my right signal, and eased to the right lane to get off the exit. I found the first open parking spot and turned the engine off. I remembered to pull the brake and then unlocked my seat belt. I noticed a building and a sign that read *Toilette*. I removed the ear bud and placed it on the dash, got out, and made my way to the door. I saw the doorway with a symbol of a woman and entered.

I walked in and almost passed out from the smell. I saw two stalls divided by a ceramic-tiled wall with no doors. There in front of me was a hole in the ground with what looked like two ceramic foot shapes on either side of the hole. I thought, *I guess that's where I'm supposed to place my feet?* Where the hell was I? In some third world country? I tried not to look down, hoped nobody else would come in and proceeded to squat. No sooner did I get finished with *evacuating my bladder* than I realized there was no toilet paper. Did I accidentally walk into the men's room? I thankfully remembered a few tissues in my pocket and was able to at least take care of the final business. I quickly zipped my jeans and ran out of the building before the smell overtook me.

I stopped and took in a deep breath of fresh air, and as I looked down, I realized I had pissed on my boots. My favorite pair of boots had spots all over them. I quickly grabbed a leaf from a tree and tried to wipe them clean, but to no avail. I shook my head as I made my way to the car and again got behind the wheel. I grabbed my purse and pulled out my waterless soap and quickly squeezed the clear liquid in my left palm and proceeded to scrub my hands.

I placed the ear bud back in and said, "What the hell kind of bathroom facility is that? I pissed all over my boots." I heard more than one chuckle in my ear, which reminded me more people were listening in on our conversation.

"Oh, I guess I forgot to tell you how the *toilettes* are in France."

"Why do I have the feeling you didn't forget? That was disgusting! Couldn't we have found a gas station somewhere?"

"No, it's too risky."

"Don't you need to use the bathroom?"

"I used that tree next to your car."

"I'd have been better off using a tree. I thought you were trying to conceal yourself?"

"Nobody saw me taking a piss. You need to relax and just get back on the highway."

I started the engine and made my way out of the parking lot and back onto the highway without any jack-rabbiting. I smiled with pride and tried to forget the hole in the floor... and my boots.

Another half hour passed, and I noticed signs for Arras. "Hey, I think we're getting close to the town of Arras."

"Aye, you need to make a left once you get off the exit. Follow that road through to the next roundabout."

It was strange talking out loud to nobody and having a conversation with someone from the tiny earpiece lodged in my ear. I continued as he instructed and felt myself more at ease driving a standard. As I approached the next roundabout, I heard him tell me to turn onto the second exit off the roundabout, and the supermarket would be on the left. My stomach started to do flip-flops again as I realized I was getting closer to the meeting point.

I turned on my left signal and pulled into the parking lot. "Okay, I'm here, now what do I do?"

"You wait until they call. I'm pulling over to the far right behind you. I have a clear view of the entire parking lot. I'll be able to hear the conversation when they call and we'll be searching the location of their signal. Try to keep them on the line as long as you can. I think this would be a good time to demand that you speak to your niece."

"I'll do the best that I can." According to the clock on the dash, I only had a few minutes until they called me again. I had a feeling they were watching me from somewhere, so I tried to act as nonchalantly as I could.

The Irish brogue once again played in my ear.

Man, his accent was sexy. "Remember to remain as calm as you can. We have eyes on you, and we'll know if anyone tries to approach the car."

A sudden thought occurred to me that if I was being watched, they might see my lips moving. I replied, keeping my lips still and said, "What if they see me talking to no one?"

"What did you say?"

Again, I tried to speak like a ventriloquist and repeated the question. He still didn't understand what I had said, so I yelled, "What if they see me talking to no one?"

"Then stop talking."

"Really, that's your answer, to stop talking?" He really knew how to get on my last nerve.

Before I could call him a jerk, my phone rang. My heart slammed in my chest, and I read Mandy's name on the screen. I carefully placed it to my earpiece ear and said, "Hello."

The voice on the other end said, "You've done very well with following instructions. I see you're alone. You have fifteen minutes to make it to the *D'amours Snack Bar*. Wait there for the next call."

"I'm not going anywhere until I talk to Mandy. Either you put her on the phone and let me know she's okay, or I'm done."

There was hesitation and some shuffling in the background before a shaky voice said, "Aunt Hannah, is that you?"

"Mandy... Mandy, are you okay? Are you hurt? Talk to me." The line went dead, and my screen went back to my recent calls list. I set the phone down on the seat and leaned my head against the steering wheel. I had no tears left in me.

I sat for another minute when I heard a cautious voice ask, "Was that your niece's voice?"

"I think so. It sounded like her, but I'm not sure. You can call her by her name. She sounded exhausted."

"You need to put your emotions aside now and make it to that restaurant. We weren't able to trace the call, but this restaurant is close to where we think Ivankov's safe house is located. You don't have a lot of time."

"I know, I know, give me a minute, okay? I'm new to this. Where do I go to find this place?" I sat back against the seat and took in a deep breath. I started the engine and ran the driving steps through my head and pulled out of the supermarket parking spot.

"Make a left at the intersection and follow that roundabout to the very next left exit. Stay on that road about four miles and then you'll make a right. I'll keep you posted when we get close to it."

I made the turn and tried not to stall the car, all the while veering from cars whizzing by me at a frantic speed. And I thought Virginians drove like maniacs! I followed the roundabout and made the left and continued up the road. I didn't even get the chance to comprehend that I was driving in France. All I could think about was Mandy's safety. I tried to observe and revel in the beauty of the lavender planted in the medians and the quaint buildings along the road. Since I couldn't read French well enough, it was hard to understand exactly what the business signs were advertising.

I was about to ask when I needed to make the next right when he said, "At the next roundabout, you'll follow it almost the whole way around and make the last right. You'll follow that road another two miles, and you'll see the *D'amours Snack Bar* on your left. I'll be right behind you, parked across the street. It's a small business."

"How much more running around will I to have to do? This is ridiculous."

"I suspect after this last stop, they'll direct you to meet Ivankov at his safe house."

I thought I heard him wrong as I made the turn into the restaurant parking lot. "What did you just say? Did you just say I'm going to be meeting Ivankov himself? You never told me I'd be meeting *him*. Why didn't you say something about that?"

The next voice I heard wasn't Finn's but agent Sliwa's. "We weren't positive you *would* meet with Ivankov until now. Don't worry, Ms Mills. We have agents all around this house."

"Oh, that makes me feel so much better." I was about to call agent Sliwa a few choice names when my cell phone rang yet again.

I tapped the phone screen and tried to listen to the next set of instructions. Sure enough, I was to meet at a house up the road and wait in the driveway. The phone disconnected and my palms were clammy, along with the back of my neck. These agents were actually going to have me meet with some Russian sicko who traffics young women, drugs, and apparently diamonds.

"Okay, so how do you all plan on protecting Mandy and me? Is that even a part of your equation?" I rubbed my temples and waited for some response.

"Hannah, we don't plan on coming out of that house without you or Mandy." Finn's voice was kind and calm. It was reassuring somehow. That was the first time he had used Mandy's first name and mine.

"Alright, so I have no blanket to give them, but I have the pink diamond. How do I explain any of that?"

Finn's voice crackled in my ear. "You can tell them you were bluffing about the blanket. Let them know they have the real deal, but then you can show Ivankov the diamond and the name we gave for the contact in the States."

"How long am I going to be in there before you come in?"

"We'll be in as soon as we hear him agree to the exchange."

I started the engine again and backed out of the confined parking lot. "Let's get this over with before I lose my nerve."

I made a right-hand turn and proceeded down the road about a mile and saw the intersection where I was to turn left. As I drove a few blocks, I spotted the house with the large iron gate and the gold medallion displaying the letters *KJM*. The gate was closed, but as I pulled closer and the nose of my car slightly touched the rails, the gate instantly opened toward the driveway.

The quaint house to my right was adorned with flower boxes filled with bright flowers on every window ledge. The landscaping was finely manicured, and there was a horse and a cow in a field next to the house, separated by a wire fence. If I were here under different circumstances, I would have loved to explore the grounds.

I pulled in and took a deep breath and again mimicked a ventriloquist and said, "I've pulled into the driveway and the gate just closed. You all better know what the hell you're doing."

I grabbed the velvet pouch with the diamond and stuffed it in the front of my bra and tucked it flat against my left breast. My left breast was a tad smaller than my right, which gave me more room to conceal the pouch. I never could figure out why my left side was smaller. I guess now wasn't the exact time to find the answer.

I opened my car door and spotted out of the corner of my left eye a very tall, burly, bald goon standing next to me. I had no idea where he came from, but I did notice the exposed pistol in the waist of his jeans when his jacket slightly moved. I tried to smile but my lips wouldn't move so I followed his nod toward a small metal door.

I grabbed the square handle and opened the door, my eyes trying to adjust to the darkness as I moved inside. After a few steps, the lights automatically turned on, and I was standing in what looked to be the basement. I felt the goon behind me as he pushed a buzzer and the wooden door in front of me opened.

My heart was pounding in my chest and I couldn't hear any noises from Finn. I certainly hoped they were all where they said they'd be as I made my way through the second door and ascended the stairs. I walked through another door and found myself in the kitchen. It was rectangular and tiny, with a small table against the right wall and a large window at the end. From there, I could see across the street to another quaint French home.

My attention moved to the right as another goon appeared from the living area. He was slightly shorter than the other goon, with the same burly frame, but he had long hair pulled back into a ponytail. He nodded his head and guided me to come into the room and sit down. Didn't any of these idiots talk?

As I made my way into the living room, I spotted a very large – no, actually he was fat – man sitting in a wooden dining chair, looking out the window. I assumed he was Ivankov. His hair was coal black and slicked back with grease against his scalp. He was smoking a cigar, which triggered my gag reflexes from the smoke that lingered in the air.

Without turning toward me, he spoke in a Russian accent and said, "Good day, Ms Mills, nice to finally meet you. Did you bring the diamond and the real blanket this time?"

I could feel the sweat dripping down between my breasts and wondered how was I going to give them a wet pouch? When I tried to speak, my mouth felt like I had eaten a cotton ball. I tried to swallow and said, "I have the diamond, but I lied about the blanket. The one I gave you is real."

His body began to shake as he let out a loud laugh. He finally turned toward me, and his gray eyes stared right into mine. "I like your tenacity, Ms Mills. You have, as you Americans say, brass balls. I like a gutsy woman. Please have a seat, and we can examine this pink diamond you claim to have."

"I'm not doing anything until I see my niece." I looked around the room and spotted a doorway toward the back of the house. "Where is she?"

"She is in the other room, and she is fine. You need not worry about her. Now please, sit down before Hugo here helps you to sit down."

I could feel *Hugo* breathing down the back of my neck, so I shifted to the right and slid into the dining chair across from Ivankov. "I think I'm at a disadvantage. You know my name, but I have no idea who you are."

He removed the slimy cigar nub and placed it into a glass ashtray. He slightly smiled and said, "I am Borya Ivankov. I am pleased to make your acquaintance. Now, let me see the diamond."

Boy, he doesn't waste any time. I suddenly realized I was going to have to get the pouch from my bra. I didn't quite think this through. I hesitated and then carefully unfastened one button on my shirt and slipped my hand in and grabbed the pouch. I placed the pouch on the table and quickly re-buttoned my shirt.

Ivankov chuckled and said, "A pretty good hiding place."

He grabbed and opened the cinched pouch and slowly let the diamond ring land in the palm of his left stubby hand. His eyes grew wide as he grasped the stone between his thumb and forefinger. He then reached into his front shirt pocket and pulled out a loupe and placed it against his right eye. He rolled the diamond between his fingers as he examined it through the molecular lens.

He gave a wide smile which revealed crusty yellow teeth, probably from smoking so many cigars, and said, "It would appear you have been telling the truth. This is indeed an authentic pink diamond. Now, who is it you know that I can do business with in these diamonds?"

Before I could reach into my pants pocket to pull out the card with the name the FBI gave to me, I heard a scuffle in the basement. Within seconds, I heard gunshots as I shot out of my chair and slid under the dining table. I could see Hugo's feet run toward the kitchen door and then saw him suddenly land on his back after a burst of shots hit him in the gut.

Ivankov got out of his chair and moved faster than I thought he possibly could and began to run to the front door. I then heard men yelling they were the FBI and the gunfire stopped. I thought this was my only chance to get Mandy, so I slid out on the other side of the table on all fours and then ran straight to the doorway I had spotted earlier.

I began opening doors into empty rooms, yelling Mandy's name. I saw a set of stairs at the end of a hall and made my way up, skipping steps two at a time. When I realized Mandy was nowhere to be found, I tried to catch my breath and flopped down on one of the beds. There, folded next to the pillow, was the First Phase blanket. I dropped my head into my hands and began to cry.

I thought I heard Finn's voice, but my head was buzzing from the gunshots, and I could feel my stomach begin to roll. I shot off the bed and ran into the bathroom and started to hurl into the toilet. Within a few seconds, I felt a large, warm hand on my shoulder and another on my forehead. I knew it was Finn from his musky cologne.

I pushed away from the toilet and sat back on my heels and leaned my cheek against the cold, tiled wall. Finn grabbed a towel and ran it under the faucet and then began to wipe my mouth. I must have looked like shit. He rinsed the towel and then began to wipe my brow. My breathing slightly relaxed as my heart slowed down to a somewhat normal rhythm.

I opened my eyes as tears began to fall down my

cheeks. I whispered, "She's not here. They lied to me again. Where is she, Finn? What did they do to her?"

Finn set the towel in the sink and grabbed my shoulders as his eyes met mine. "I'm not sure, Hannah. But why don't we head downstairs and try to see if we can find out? Are you able to stand?"

"Yeah, I think I'm done making a fool of myself."

I let him pull me up as I steadied myself against the wall to make sure my legs were solid and that I didn't need to hurl again. I slowly made my way into the back bedroom and grabbed the blanket. It served no purpose for me anymore, but it was mine, and I planned on taking it back.

We slowly walked down the stairs and out of the house. Finn directed me to sit on the bench in the garden as he walked over to Ivankov and began interrogating him. After half an hour, Finn walked over and sat next to me on the bench.

"Hannah, he said they already sold her off to another prostitution ring two days ago. He said it was to another Russian who works in the south of France. I have an address."

I swiftly moved my gaze from my feet and stared into his green Irish eyes. "Then we have to find her. You can all use your expertise and help me find her."

The familiar voice came from my right. "We're not going to spend our time chasing after your niece."

CHAPTER EIGHT

I LOOKED UP AND STARED AT AGENT SLIWA. "What the hell do you mean you're not going to help me find my niece?"

"We got what we came for. We've been tracking Ivankov for two years. There may even be a promotion in it for me." Sliwa slapped his hand on Finn's back and said, "As far as I'm concerned, Finn, she's your problem now. We don't care what she did in the States. She held up her end of the bargain."

I watched as agent Sliwa walked away and I turned my attention to Finn. "I can't leave her here. God only knows what she's gone through. Please, don't take me back to the States without her. I promise I'll take what's coming to me, but don't leave her out there alone, being used for sex. She just turned twenty-one. I thought you made me a promise. I know you never said it, but I thought we had an agreement."

Finn smiled and placed his hand on my knee. "Your commitment to Mandy is refreshing, and yes, we may not have a written agreement, but I do believe I owe it to you to help find her. You're still in my custody. I need to talk to my boss. You still robbed a bank, Hannah."

I felt my heart leap as I wrapped my arms around his neck. "Thank you. You don't know how much this means to me."

"I think I do. Your niece is lucky to have you." He stood up and grabbed my elbow and guided me toward his car. I sensed he felt awkward after my hug, but he didn't pull away or seem to mind, which was interesting.

I watched the agents take Ivankov and his men away in handcuffs. It actually felt pretty good to be a part of having these assholes arrested, but it didn't solve me finding Mandy. I realized I was going to need to make a phone call to my brother. I completely lost track of time, and he'd be sick with worry.

I squeezed the blanket to my chest and remembered my camera. I set the blanket down on the front seat of Finn's nondescript black sedan and made my way to the rental car I had driven. I opened the door and grabbed the camera off the floor. My instincts kicked in and I began to take pictures of Ivankov and his men being loaded up in a van. I zoomed in and caught the eyes of Ivankov through the lens. He was glaring back at me, and an immediate chill ran down my back.

I ignored the look and continued to take pictures when Ivankov yelled over to me in his Russian accent, "I would stop taking those pictures if I were you."

For some reason, I felt sassy and brave, and said, "Why is that?"

"Because this isn't over and we don't forget. You do anything with those pictures, and you'll point and shoot for the last time."

"Is that a threat?"

Finn broke the conversation and shoved Ivankov into the back of the van and slammed the door shut. He walked toward me and said, "I think you'd better put the camera down before Sliwa takes it from you."

I slipped the camera behind my back and then quickly got into the car. I hid the camera under the blanket and as I waited for Finn, I spotted my purse on the back seat and began to rummage for my phone and saw the battery was dead. How was I going to contact my brother?

Finn got behind the wheel and looked over at me and said, "My boss has given me the go-ahead to find Mandy. I think they're riding high on this bust. He hasn't forgotten that you've committed a federal crime, but he feels we owe this to you to help find her."

I let out a sigh of relief and dropped my head back against the seat. "That's great news, I really appreciate it. Do you have any way for me to charge my phone?"

He leaned over and opened the glove box and pulled out an adapter that plugged into the cigarette lighter. His elbow brushed against my knee as he quickly handed it to me. "Here, do you have a cable?"

I ignored the heat that ran up my leg and through my unmentionable parts and said, "Yeah, and thanks. I'd like to call my brother. I really think he needs to know what's going on, but I don't want to jack up my phone bill more than it already is."

"You can use mine, but what exactly are you going to tell him?"

"I need to tell him the truth, but I'm not exactly

sure if that's a good idea. I'm still trying to figure out how Mandy got hooked up with these jerks."

"Ivankov told Sliwa that one of his men was in the States, out at a bar looking for candidates to sell, when he ran into your niece. She obviously fell for his charm and after a few drinks, she spilled the information about the blanket that her aunt had received and told them the possible value. It was just an added bonus."

"Oh Mandy, she always did talk too much." My stomach started to rumble, and it was clear that Finn heard it.

"I think we need to find a place to get something to eat. There's a restaurant on the way, about a mile or so down the road."

"Where exactly are we going?"

"We are going to Nice, which is located in the Southeast coast of France on the Mediterranean Sea."

"We're going to Nice? I've always wanted to visit there, but obviously under better circumstances."

Finn started the engine and pulled out of the parking area and through the gate. He made a left and shifted into second, and we were on our way. For the first time, I had the chance to really look at the landscape along the road. It was picturesque, similar to what we have back home, but clearly flatter. There were open farm fields with rolled bales of hay strewn across the meadows, and fields with cows and horses grazing together. The lavender was in full bloom and planted everywhere, giving off its pungent fragrance.

Within a few minutes, Finn pulled into another parking area that looked like a strip mall. He pointed to an establishment with a green sign that read *Le Potager Des Demoiselles*. From what I could remember from my French class, it meant the kitchen garden of ladies. I needed to brush up on the verb and adjectives, because that made no sense to me.

I nodded and got out of the car and followed him to the door. "So, do you know anything about this place, or was this a random pick?"

Finn held the door open and said, "I got a few tips from a few of the agents. I think you'll enjoy the food here."

As I entered the restaurant, I noticed the bright, clean marble floors with bistro-style tables and chairs precisely placed throughout the room. It was small and quaint, with rows of wine bottles neatly stacked in shelves along the walls. It seemed informal in a classic chic sort of way. There was a wall of windows and beyond that an outdoor seating area covered by a circus-like tent.

Finn caught the eye of a beautiful woman of about thirty or so, with short, cropped blonde hair and bulging breasts popping out of her white cotton, button-down shirt. I couldn't take my eyes off her chest. It was like a magnet pulling me right in, and apparently Finn couldn't take his eyes off, either.

She met us with a gorgeous bright smile and said, "*Bonjour, bienvenue à Le Potager Des Demoiselles.*"

Before I could respond, Finn broke out into an all-out conversation and had the blonde bombshell laughing and touching his arm as she directed us to a table at the far end of the restaurant. She winked at me and then handed us menus. There were a few more exchanged words as she left and Finn began to peruse the menu.

He sensed my stare as his gaze slowly moved up to mine. "I know a little French."

"A little? Seriously, I think you know more than a little."

"Do you speak the language?"

"I only had a year in high school and another year in college. I was able to make out a few words. Apparently she enjoys your flattery."

Finn chuckled and continued reading the menu. I was able to decipher a few words and decided on a burger and frites, or, as we Americans say, french fries. We placed our orders while I tried not to up-chuck over Finn and Ms Frenchy's amorous exchanges. I took a sip of water and tried to ignore the silence between us, which made me very anxious.

Finn broke the silence and said, "Aren't you going to call your brother?"

"I'm trying to gather up enough courage. Plus, I think I need something to eat before I call him. I'm going to need all the strength I can get to tell him about Mandy. I'm not even sure how I'm going to do it."

Ms Frenchy brought our food, and I was pleasantly surprised that Finn never took his eyes from me when he said, "I can make the call."

"You? You're going to make the call? Why would you do that?"

"Sure, because I think your brother would be a little more receptive hearing about his daughter from me."

I bit into a french fry, which immediately made my head swoon, and I forgot what I was going to say. "This has to be the best french fry I've ever eaten." I opened my eyes and saw his right eyebrow raised, and I remembered where I was. "Sorry, I'm just starving, and this really is good."

"My steak is pretty good also."

I remembered his offer and said, "Thank you for offering to speak to my brother. I think I'll take you up on that. I don't even know where to begin, and you'd be able to talk your FBI jargon and come off better than me telling him Mandy was kidnapped and sold into prostitution." As soon as I said the words, my stomach did a flip-flop, and suddenly I wasn't hungry anymore.

Finn set down his steak knife and took a sip of Chardonnay. "You can't dwell on that, so come on, finish eating. We really are in a time crunch. As soon as we're finished, I'll give him a call."

I nodded my head and took a huge bite out of the burger. The food just seemed to taste better in France. I watched Finn skillfully cut his steak, and I began to wonder if he was skillful in everything he did. Then I decided to stop thinking about his skills in bed and switched my thoughts to my burger.

We finished our meals, Finn paid, and we both used the bathroom facilities. We went outside to stretch our legs while Finn made the dreaded phone call. I watched him pace back and forth, waving his arm and then stop in mid-stride and run his hand through his hair. It was pretty obvious he was trying to convey everything to Justin. I felt my neck get hot and perspiration began to drip down my back.

Finn finished the conversation and walked over to me by the car. "That's that, I've explained everything to your brother."

"And?"

"And he's quite distraught. He was pissed at you at first until I explained how this all got started."

"Did you tell him I robbed a bank?"

"Apparently that was all over the news."

I almost lost my balance as I whipped my head around to face him and said, "It's all over the news? Are you kidding me? Oh my gosh, my parents are never going to let me live this down."

Finn placed his hand on my shoulder. "Justin understands why you robbed the bank. He found it quite amusing and honorable that you did it to save Mandy. He knows how much you love her and would probably give your life for her. He's going to explain everything to your parents. Now come on, we really need to make some time. It's quite a few hours to Nice."

I shook my head and opened my car door, slumped into the seat, and buckled my belt. Finn did the same and started the engine. Again, we were rolling down the main road. I had to admit the last forty-eight hours had been such a whirlwind, I didn't allow my mind to go to that dark place where Mandy was, or what happened to her. It made me sick to my stomach and now that Justin knew, it made the situation all the more difficult.

I tried to refocus and turned to look out the window. "How long a drive do we have?"

"It's about a nine- or ten-hour drive."

"How are we even going to know if Mandy is still in Nice? We've already lost so much time."

"The information Ivankov gave me leads me to believe they're planning on staying there awhile."

"Who is it that has her this time?"

"Vladislav Dubsky, who is also a known drug and human trafficker. He's been off the radar for some time."

"So I've been able to surface two assholes that the FBI has been trying to arrest."

Finn glanced over at me, and I could feel the weight of his stare. "Aye, you have, but that doesn't change anything in your situation. I know you're thinking this may play a part in keeping you out of jail. But as soon as we find Mandy, and we will, I'm taking you back to the States to stand trial. It'll be up to a judge to decide your fate."

"Gee, and here I thought you were starting to like me." I grabbed the lever on my seat and leaned back and closed my eyes. I was exhausted, and my stomach was full, which was a perfect combination for a nap. My head weaved and bobbed to the swaying of the car, and eventually, I was lulled to sleep.

My body jolted to the left and I opened my eyes in fear and discovered the day had turned into night. The car had stopped and I tried to sit up and stretch my neck, which apparently had been stuck in the same position for the entire time I slept. I also felt dampness on my chin and realized, yet again, I had drooled all over myself. I quickly wiped it with the back of my hand only to find Finn laughing.

"What's so funny?"

"Did you know that you talk in your sleep?"

"I do not."

"And you drool."

I gave him one of my glares and adjusted the seat into an upright position. "Why have we stopped? Where are we?"

"We've stopped because I'm exhausted, and I found us a hotel to stay for the night. We can get a good night's rest and start fresh in the morning."

According to my Fossil rose gold watch it was

nine-thirty. "I don't want to waste any more time. We need to keep going. What town are we in? How far do we have to go?"

"Do you always talk this much and ask a ton of questions? We're in the town of Lyon, and this is a hotel. You've had the luxury of sleeping all this time, but I haven't. I need a bed and a shower."

"It looks kind of cheesy."

"It's affordable, only fifty euro a night. Now, our room is on the third floor, room thirty-two."

"*Our* room? What do you mean, our room? For fifty euro a night you couldn't get separate rooms?"

"I'm not letting you out of my sight, and besides, there are two double beds. Now let's go, I'm ready for some shut-eye." Finn reached around to the back seat and grabbed a duffle bag.

"Where would I run off to?"

He gave no reply as my stomach did that weird flinch, along with other parts of my body. Why was I suddenly envisioning him naked in the shower? I shook my head and got out of the car and then opened the back door to get my suitcase and camera. I followed him into the hotel and felt as if everyone was staring at us. Like they knew we were staying at the hotel in sin. I could see my mother rolling her eyes now.

"What'd you sign us in as, Mr and Mrs Smith?"

"No, Mr and Mrs MacNally."

"That's not funny."

"It wasn't meant to be."

We got into the elevator and Finn was wearing his usual sexy smirk. I wasn't in the mood for any more arguing so I stared at the numbers as they lit up in sequence until we landed on number three. The doors opened, and I stepped out into the hall and looked to the left and spotted an arrow pointing to rooms numbered thirty to thirty-eight.

I pulled my suitcase behind me and made my way down the hall. When we arrived at number thirty-two, Finn slipped the key card out of the pouch and inserted it into the door. He pushed down on the handle and held it open for me to enter. I guess his mother taught him some manners.

The room actually looked pretty clean. The walls were painted beige, and the carpet was brown. The beds seemed firm enough and the bathroom was encircled with cinnamon ceramic tile on the floor and shower.

I slid my suitcase next to the bed by the window and pulled up the comforter and yanked the corner of the sheet and began inspecting the mattress. I could feel Finn staring at me, and without looking up, I said, "Checking for bed bugs. Looks like it's okay."

He shook his head and dropped his duffle bag on the bed and unzipped the top compartment. He began to pull some items out and walked toward the bathroom. "I'll take a shower first if you don't mind. I figure you need more time than me, so I'd like to get in before it's morning again."

"You're just full of jokes tonight, aren't you? That's fine; I'll just wait and watch some television. Are there any English-speaking shows on in France?"

He gave me that 'are you kidding?' look, and walked into the bathroom. I heard him turn on the shower and I tried to ignore my thoughts of him undressing and lathering his six pack abs. As I tried to flip through the stations, I noticed steam slipping out through the door and caught the reflection of the bathroom in the mirror. He had left the door open a few inches, and I had a nice view of the shower door.

I averted my eyes and tried to focus on a woman interviewing another woman at a grocery store. I heard the shower stop, and I couldn't keep from looking in the mirror. There in front of me was Finn's firm ass facing me as he maneuvered the towel across his back. There went the twinge again in my genitals. I stood up and moved to the chair by the desk and pretended to be engrossed in the television show. I heard the door open as Finn stepped out in a pair of navy running shorts and a gray Nike t-shirt.

He chuckled and said, "Taking in the news?"

I glanced over and watched him continue to towel off his hair. "I was trying to see how much French I could pick up."

"I see. Well, you can have the bathroom now."

I rolled my eyes and grabbed my makeup bag, my sweats, and a nightshirt. "Why is it women get a bad rap for taking too long in the bathroom?"

I escaped into the bathroom and made sure to close the door. There wasn't any lock, so I rolled a hand towel and propped it on the floor against the door. Not sure what that was going to do, but it would at least let me know if he snuck a peek.

I took a quick shower, dried my hair, and brushed my teeth. I noticed the towel hadn't moved, so I kicked it out of the way and opened the door. Finn was already lying in bed with the remote in his hand, watching soccer. At least I thought it was soccer.

I placed my makeup bag and dirty clothes back in the suitcase and swiftly slipped under the covers. I propped up my pillows and said, "Will you be watching this for much longer?"

Finn hit the button on the remote, and the television went off. "Nope, we have a long day ahead of us."

The room was dark, and I could hear him shift in the bed and all was quiet. *Okay then, I guess that's it, time for bed*, I thought. I pulled the covers under my chin and closed my eyes. My groin had calmed down as I tried to ignore my mind's eye vision of Finn's ass. What type of exercise did he do to keep it so firm? Okay, if I was going to get any sleep I needed to think of something else. I took a deep breath and squeezed another pillow under my arms and eventually drifted off to sleep.

CHAPTER NINE

My heart was racing, and I could barely breathe as I ran toward the door. I could feel the tears slipping down my cheeks and the sweat beading on my forehead. I tried to grab her, but her hand kept slipping out of mine. Her grip slid and broke free from mine as she fell into the shadow of darkness.

I felt a hard squeeze on my shoulder when my eyes flew open and there in front of me on my bed was Finn. I saw his lips move, but I couldn't make out his words. I tried to clear my head and said, "What are you doing on my bed?"

"I think you were having a dream, or a nightmare. Are you okay?"

I sat up and leaned against the headboard and wiped the tears from my cheek. Those were real. "I'm not sure. I think I was dreaming about Mandy."

Finn stood up from the bed and fumbled with the comforter that had caught on his foot. He tried to keep his balance and composure and said, "I figured as much. You called her name out a few times."

I felt my heart beating in my throat and tried to remain calm. "What time is it?"

"It's half past seven. We really need to get a move on. There's a café across the street. I thought we could go there for breakfast."

I wearily pushed away the covers and slid my legs out of bed and onto the floor. "Yeah, let me use the bathroom and change. I'll be right out."

He reached out and touched my elbow and said, "We're going to find her, Hannah."

I smiled and then noticed what I thought was a large bulge in his shorts. He spotted my stare and quickly turned and walked over to the window. My face got hot as I fumbled through my suitcase and grabbed another pair of jeans and a lightweight beige sweater. I bolted to the bathroom and shut the door behind me. Did he have a hard-on? Is that what I saw? I suddenly felt quite proud of myself and started to brush my teeth.

I then glanced into the mirror and thought, wait a minute, what if that was just the normal morning wake-up hard-on men get? I felt my spirits drop and continued to get dressed and put on my makeup. Either way, I think he was embarrassed. Better to let this awkward moment pass.

I stepped out of the bathroom and saw that he was already dressed, with his duffle bag closed and on the bed. I threw my things back into the suitcase and zipped it shut. I casually smiled and followed him out of the room. As we made our way back into the elevator, neither of us said a word. It was driving me crazy wondering what he was thinking. Man, this was awkward.

The elevator landed on the ground floor lobby, and the doors opened. Finn walked over to the desk and handed the key card to the young man with dark-rimmed glasses and curly brown hair. He took his receipt and nodded his head toward me and then toward the door. I guess we were continuing our day in silence. Yep, I was now convinced his hard-on wasn't the usual wake-up call.

I tried to conceal my grin as I walked out of the hotel and into the crisp morning air. He popped open the trunk and dropped my suitcase inside and then shut the lid. We walked over to the café in silence and grabbed coffee and crêpes to go. The order was ready very quickly; I guess the sight of Finn's FBI badge helped speed up the employee working the counter.

I got back into the front passenger seat and locked my belt. I tried to remain calm and collected as he got in and threw his duffle bag in the backseat, buckled his belt, and started the engine. I knew we had about five more hours before we reached Nice, so I figured I'd better come up with something to talk about.

"What part of Ireland are you from?"

He grunted, "County Cork."

"Where is that, exactly?"

"It's the southernmost county in Ireland. The actual town I grew up in was Ballincolig. It's considered one of the largest towns in the county."

I could sense his ease so I thought it was safe to continue asking him questions. I also couldn't deny I was curious. "What was it like growing up there?"

"It has history of the Gunpowder Mills, a library, a multiplex cinema, playgrounds, shopping centers, and a large park. Nothing more needed for a kid to grow up there." He shifted into third and took the roundabout toward the A7.

I tried to keep from hitting my head on the window as we raced the circle and made the turn. I shoved a piece of crêpe into my mouth before he made another turn. "Did you always want to be an agent?"

"Aye, I knew from the age of sixteen."

Now that statement was spoken with pride. I glanced over and caught his smirk. "Yeah, I always knew I wanted to be a photographer. I just can't seem to make any money at it."

"Hence, the bank robbery in Sharpsburg."

"Yes, and a whole lot of other issues."

Finn adjusted the rearview mirror and then rested his hand on the gearshift. "So how much is that blanket worth?"

"I was told close to a million. It could go for more at auction. My Great Aunt Dorothy left it to me after she passed away, which ticked off my mother. I'm not really sure what I want to do with it now. It's brought on all of this mess." I looked out the window and tried to suppress the thoughts that were running in and out of my mind, but I had to know Finn's thoughts about Mandy. "I've avoided this question for the last two days, but do you think they've had Mandy *doing* things against her will?"

Finn's jaw tightened, and his eyes squinted. "I think I'd rather not answer that question. Honestly, I have no idea. They may be saving her for someone, which is why we need to get to Nice sooner rather than later. Someone may have already *used* her, but I think you need to keep your mind from going there."

"Yeah, I've been avoiding those thoughts, but sometimes it creeps up on me. I feel like this is entirely my fault."

"It's only natural for you to take the blame, but you need to move on from that self-guilt. It gets you nowhere. So, tell me about this photography business of yours. From some of the photographs I've seen, you have a good eye for detail."

I moved my gaze from the landscape whizzing by me, took another bite of a crêpe, and looked at Finn. I appreciated him trying to change the subject. I liked that about him, along with his sexy physique and gorgeous eyes. "Thanks. My professors used to tell me that. I have a small studio in town, walking distance from my place. One of my mom's realtor friends lets me use it for free. She takes pity on me."

"Never turn down a pity gift."

"That's what I always say. Of course, my brother is usually the one giving me the pity gifts. I really owe him big, especially now." I didn't feel like talking anymore about my life. It was too depressing... and embarrassing. "So how did you end up becoming an agent and working in the States?"

"My family moved to Sacramento, California, when I was fifteen. My dad was a solicitor and for some reason fell in love with California while on a business trip. My mom fell in love with the weather. She never could handle the cold rains." Finn glanced over at me and then moved his eyes back on the road. "After looking into all that was needed to move to the States, my parents became citizens, and because of the law changing in 2001, I automatically became a citizen because my parents were naturalized. The family back in Ireland pretty much shunned us, but it felt right to my parents. It was a long process, but we never looked back."

"Don't you miss Ireland?"

"Aye, and I've been back on occasion."

"How did you become an FBI agent?"

"I got my degree in political science and then went into the police academy. From there, I've moved into the undercover operations."

"Where did you learn French?"

"I had a year in high school and then two years in college. It comes in handy in quite a few of my cases. Being multilingual is part of the requirements. I also know a little Russian and Spanish."

"And then you got pulled into chasing after me."

Finn glanced over at me and gave me that same sexy smirk, which sent my groin area into a tailspin. "It's been an interesting ride, Hannah Mills."

The lull of his sexy Irish accent saying my name could make me do just about anything. I tried to slow down my heart and quickly crossed my legs. I think I could have had an orgasm right on the spot. "So you said you hadn't found the right woman, but I'm sure you've dated some, no?"

"Aye, I have dated... some, but it takes up a lot of my time, and very few understand the commitment I have to the job. But I make out okay." Finn's smile softened his face as he continued to watch the road ahead of us and popped a piece of a crêpe into his mouth.

I felt like I had pried enough into his life. I wanted to know more about this sexy Irish FBI agent, but I had to remember the reason I was here. No matter how hard I tried, I couldn't keep my mind from drifting to Mandy. As much as I enjoyed talking with Finn, I decided to shut down my mind and find a diversion.

I looked at my watch and saw we had driven for a couple of hours. We ran out of things to say, so I reached around to the back seat and grabbed my camera. I always felt safe behind the lens. I looked out the window and decided to capture the beauty of France before this nightmare was over.

It surprised me to see how the landscape changed from northern France to the southern side. It was quite flat in Arras, but I could see the gradual change of a few more mountains beginning to appear. I set my camera to the appropriate shutter speed and began shooting. I took picture after picture, catching the charming scenery. I could always lose myself behind the camera. It somehow found a way to lift my spirits.

Finn asked, "Do you always have your camera with you?"

I answered without taking my eye off the viewfinder and said, "Absolutely, it's a part of me. I do some of my best work spontaneously."

"You definitely caught a few good pics of Ivankov's men. That's what led to his arrest."

"If you don't mind, I'd rather not talk about any of that right now. I need a diversion, and this is usually what helps." I continued taking pictures and thought, *I hope he doesn't think I'm rude, but I'm not in the mood to think about why I'm here.*

"I understand. Everyone needs a diversion. I usually run first thing in the morning, but haven't had the chance the last few days."

I guess he's not done talking. I took my eye away from the camera and sat straight back into my seat and began to look through the photos I'd caught. The silence was awkward again, so I said, "I also do yoga. That helps, along with meditation. I haven't had the chance to do any of that, either. Taking pictures helps, though."

"Everyone needs an outlet." Finn turned on his signal and moved into the right lane. "We're going to need some petrol. You can use the *toilette* if you need."

I wasn't going to complain about the stop. I did need to *use the toilette*. Talking to strangers about bodily functions was funny. Everyone's so prim and proper. Why not just say 'I need to take a piss'? Just then Finn looked at me, and I really had to think if I'd just said that out loud. He pulled next to a pump and turned off the engine. He didn't respond so I assumed I was safe.

I set my camera on the floor in front of me and tucked it under my hoodie and got out of the car. I wasn't really hungry but decided I should get something to eat, anyway, when I realized I had no money.

"I was thinking of getting a little something to eat. Were you hungry at all?"

Finn finished pumping the gas and set the nozzle back into the pump. "Not really, but I may get something."

I stood there staring at him, waiting for him to catch a clue and said, "I don't have any money."

"Aye, I got your meaning by the glare you just gave me."

I didn't glare at him... did I? I shifted my feet and said, "Sorry, my emotions tend to stand out on my face sometimes."

"Let me pull up to a spot and let this guy behind me get some petrol. You go ahead in and I'll meet you in there."

I did as he instructed, grabbed my purse, and made my way into the convenient store and saw the sign for *toilette* and then the symbol for women posted on the wall. I held my breath as I walked in and was thrilled to see regular enclosed bathroom stalls. No more standing over a hole and peeing. In fact, it was immaculate and smelled like baby powder.

I finished relieving myself and then ventured over to the sink and unfortunately looked in the mirror. Wow! I quickly washed my hands and then proceeded to add some foundation under my eyes to cover the dark circles and added some of my Plum Fury red lipstick to my lips. Hopefully, that helped me look a little more alive.

As I placed my makeup bag back into my purse, my hand rubbed against something soft. I rooted around and pulled it out, and there between my fingertips was Mandy's small velvet satchel, which held a tiny bottle of her Cotton Candy perfume. I forgot I had it in there. She needed me to keep it for her when we were in her backyard pretending to plant pansies. Who needed perfume planting flowers? Mandy did. I had slipped it in my pocket and took it home with me by accident. I meant to give it to her, but apparently forgot. I placed it back into my purse and tried to keep the tears from welling up in the rims of my eyes. Geez, I just put on foundation.

I went back into the stall, grabbed some toilet paper, wiped the corners of my eyes and then left the restroom. I spotted Finn over by the fruit and yogurt section, and I rolled my eyes. Don't tell me he's a health freak?

I went directly to the cookie aisle and tried to figure out what the ingredients were in French. I found a pack of what looked like butter cookies and then grabbed a pack of gum. I decided I needed some caffeine and looked around for coffee. I didn't see any coffee area like you usually see in the States, but I spotted a machine that read *Café* and walked over to determine what it cost. Before I could turn around to find Finn, I felt someone behind me.

"I suppose you need money for this, too?"

There went my groin area again. Without turning around I said, "Yes, if that's not a bother."

Finn fished around in his pocket and slipped the coins in the slot. "How do you take it?"

"Regular with cream."

He pushed the buttons and we both watched the cup fall down into its placeholder as the coffee and cream mixture dumped into the paper mug. When it was finished, I slid the tiny plastic door up and grabbed the hot coffee, which almost burned my hand.

Finn looked at my cookies and shook his head. "Is that all you're going to get?"

"It'll hold me over. I see you got some fruit and yogurt."

"Aye, plus some crackers and cheese, as well. You're welcome to any of this if you like."

"Thanks, I may try some of the cheese and crackers."

We walked to the counter and waited as the tall, dark and handsome young man rang us up. He placed our purchases into a bag and handed Finn the change. As we walked away, I happened to glance back just as the hunk winked at me. I gave him a coy smile and continued out the door. I was apparently still wearing a grin because Finn was standing there with a blank face.

"Do you always make a habit of flirting with strange men?"

I thought it was pretty funny that he would even question me, as I gave him the same coy smile and said, "Only when I feel like it, and when they're as good-looking as he was."

Finn shook his head and opened his car door and slammed down into his seat. I tried to contain my laughter as I followed suit and carefully placed my coffee in the cup holder of the console. We both buckled our seat belts and remained in silence as he backed out of the parking spot, and we made our way back to the highway.

I grabbed my bag of cookies and carefully opened the end. I slid one of the buttery shortbread cookies out and popped it into my mouth. It was delicious. It sort of reminded me of the trefoil Girl Scout cookies I used to sell as a kid. Suddenly, my mind drifted to more carefree days when I was a Girl Scout. Of course, the next thought was of my girlfriend Trudy and me getting in trouble for smoking in the bathroom where our meetings took place. *I wonder where Trudy is now?*

I heard Finn bite into his apple and I started to feel guilty that I was eating cookies instead of a healthy snack. That quickly faded as I ate another cookie. I took a sip of coffee and wondered how far away we were from Nice. I missed the last signpost that marked the mileage. Of course, I didn't quite know how to convert kilometers to miles.

"How much longer do we have to go?"

Finn took another bite of his apple and wiped the juice on his sleeve. "We've only got about an hour until we're there. I may need you to plug in the address on the GPS."

"Where is the address?"

"It's on a piece of paper in my left shirt pocket."

I set my coffee back in the cup holder and reached over to his pocket. Of course, I had to reach across his chest and my elbow and forearm felt the muscles bulging out from his shirt. He smelled great and felt warm. My hand started to shake as I reached into the pocket in search of the paper. I found the corner and was trying to pull it out as fast as I could when I caught his eyes glance down to my chest.

Our eyes met, and I gave him a timid smile and said, "Got it."

"Yes, you do."

I felt heat start to radiate down my neck, and as I sat back into my seat, I felt my nipples get hard. I quickly tried to shift my arms in such a way to hide them, but it wasn't working. I willed my mind to make them soften and tried to distract myself by opening the paper and entering the address into the GPS.

Once I finished entering the address, I set the paper in the little compartment next to the gearshift. I wasn't about to put it back in his pocket, although I wouldn't have minded feeling his chest again. My nipples finally calmed down, and I decided to concentrate on my cookies as I looked out the window and pretended my heart wasn't pounding in my chest.

CHAPTER TEN

I had finished my cookies and some of Finn's cheese and crackers and realized we should be close to our destination. Sure enough, I spotted a sign showing that Nice was only two kilometers away. I turned to Finn as he began to move over into the right lane.

"Guess we're getting close." I shifted my seatbelt and reached for my camera.

"Aye, if you need to make a pit stop, we can do that here. Otherwise, I'll turn on the GPS to find the street address."

"I think I'm okay for now. What exactly is the plan, by the way?"

Finn looked over at me and then back at the road. "I've a few ideas, but we'll need to get a little settled in before we approach Dubsky."

"Settled in? How are we going to do that?" I saw the exit sign for Nice and started to take pictures. Not really sure why, it was just habit.

"I'm going to need to get the feel of their hideout and learn the comings and goings of his men. We can't just barge in. We need to be sure Mandy is there." Finn turned on the right turn signal and made his way off the ramp.

"Again, how are we going to do that?"

"We'll have a place to stay that's close, but at a distance to watch any activity that takes place."

"Like a stake-out? Oh wow, I can't wait to do that. Can we get some doughnuts and whatever healthy food you want?"

Finn raised his right eyebrow and shook his head. "What is it with people thinking we eat doughnuts on a stake-out?"

We both heard the woman's voice state we were only ten meters to our destination. Finn canceled the GPS and slowly made his way up a hill. I immediately grabbed my camera and had started to take pictures when Finn grabbed it out of my hand and set it on his lap.

"What'd you do that for?"

Finn jammed his finger over his lips and then pointed to a concrete wall to our right. "There's the house, behind that wall down the hillside."

There it stood, a white contemporary villa, which looked similar in architecture to Franklin Lloyd Wright's Darwin D. Martin House in Buffalo, NY, with phenomenal views of the Riviera. I lost my breath looking at the sea and the beautifully manicured landscape.

As Finn continued to drive by, I caught a glimpse of the sun's reflection off a rectangular lap pool at the back of the house set in a concrete deck that extended out over the mountainside.

"This place must be worth a few million."

Finn chuckled and said, "More like six million or so."

We made our way to the end of the street and took a left and slowly drove around the block. Finn pulled over into an open spot along the sidewalk and turned off the engine. He reached around to the back seat and grabbed his duffle bag and proceeded to root around in the side pocket and pulled out a business-card-sized leather case.

I wondered what he was searching for and got tired of waiting in silence. "What are you looking for?"

"I have a point of contact written down on one of these business cards." He shuffled through the cards and stopped at one and turned it over. "This is it."

"Who is this point of contact supposed to be, and what are they going to do for us now?"

Finn set the card on the dash and slipped the leather case back into the duffle bag pocket. "You ask a lot of questions. I don't know who this gentleman is, but I was given the name and address from headquarters. He should be able to give us a safe place to stay in the vicinity."

"Good, because I'm ready to eat, I'm starving." I instinctively picked up my camera and began to take pictures of the neighborhood.

"What are you taking pictures of now?"

"I don't know. It's a habit of mine. You never know when you'll catch something or someone. Look how well I did at the Eiffel Tower." I smugly smiled and tried to ignore his stare. I could see him out of the corner of my eye, which created the same trickle of heat down my neck.

I tried to focus my eye through the lens and ignore the heat ebbing its way down to my pelvic region. I focused my sight on beautiful palm trees and an orange tree in one of the high-class neighborhood homes. I noticed a pine tree and one that was similar to topiary on a larger scale. The houses were all magnificent, and it was apparent we were in one hell of an affluent neighborhood, which sat up on one big-ass mountainside.

I heard Finn start the engine as I settled back into my seat and set the camera on my lap. "So where are we headed?"

"We're going to find this address and reach out to an Adrien Dubois. Let's hope he's home."

"Why not call him?"

"My unit already contacted him."

He pulled out onto the street and made his way to the end of the block. I glanced at the houses as we drove by and felt the warm sun on my face. I opened the window and let the breeze brush my hair and skin. Just for a few seconds, I was able to relish the beauty of nature.

We made another turn and, as Finn slowed down, he pointed to a building that looked like an embassy, or a palace. "What the hell is this place?"

"This is the address of Adrien Dubois."

"Is he the Prime Minister, or a relative of the Prime Minister? This place is massive."

Finn turned into the parking lot across from the enormous concrete structure, which faced the sea, parked the car and said, "This is actually the Negresco Hotel, which is a historical monument, and has been converted to apartments."

"It doesn't look like any apartment building I've ever seen."

I opened the door, tried not to fall backward from looking up at the top of the building and gawked at the pink dome. I turned and faced the sea and watched the street-lined palm trees sway in the gentle breeze. There were tons of people of all shapes and sizes wearing bathing suits and sitting on the narrow beach under umbrellas.

I turned and followed Finn into the grand entryway of tall pillars supporting an oversized roof and balcony made of concrete. We walked through the massive doorway and into what I assumed was the foyer... for a palace.

Inside, the floor was marble, as well as the pillars, that ran in a circle around me exposing magnificent oil paintings on the walls. There was a tall staircase to the front and a massive chandelier over my head. This looked like something out of a fairytale story. I waited for a prince to come down on his white horse and carry me away.

Finn tapped my shoulder and nodded toward the elevator. "Adrien lives on the fifth floor."

We entered the elevator as Finn hit the number five button and I tried to ignore our skewed reflections in the mirrors, which reminded me of the hall of mirrors found at a carnival. The elevator stopped as it dinged on the fifth floor and the doors glided open. Even the elevator was classy.

We stepped into the luxurious hall and made our way to a door displaying the glamorous golden numbers 521. Finn knocked, and we waited. I glanced up and down the hall and admired the lavish architecture and framed art. It felt more like a museum than a place to live.

I heard the clicking of a deadbolt and then, after a few more releases of locks, the door opened. Standing in the doorway was a very tall, slender, distinguished-looking gentleman with salt and pepper hair. He smiled at us and then opened the door wide.

"Welcome to my home. You must be Agent Mc-Nally and Ms Mills. Please come in."

Finn allowed me to enter first and my eyes instantly landed on the view of the sea through the tall window at the other side of the living room. It was breathtaking. I stood off to the left and perused the oversized white plush couch and chair with matching ottoman. The floor was polished oak parquet with a unique mosaic design at the center. The kitchen was tiny but modern, and the dining set was made of cherry. It was elegant, and apparently this Adrien Dubois had money.

Adrien guided us toward the living room couch and waved his arm to join him. "Please have a seat and tell me a little about why you are here. The agency only gave me a few details."

His broken English was divine with the lilt of the French accent. He wore a gold pinky ring with a ruby stone. He had a great smile and crystal blue eyes. His oxford baby-blue shirt was crisply ironed, as well as his khaki pants. He directed his attention to Finn as I sat back and tried to conceal my stomach from rumbling again. I hadn't realized we were that close to dinner.

Finn gestured toward me and said, "Hannah's niece, Mandy, was abducted from the States by the Russian drug king and human trafficker, Borya Ivankov, and brought to Paris. Hannah was able to find a lead by a photo she had taken. We traced Borya in Arras, but unfortunately, Mandy was not there. She had been traded off to Vladislav Dubsky. We hope to be able to learn if she is still with Dubsky."

Adrien looked at me and warmly smiled. "Vladislav has been able to slip under the radar with his charm, wit, and money. If you're able to catch him with your niece, it would mean taking down a major player out of human trafficking. However, we cannot do any of that on an empty stomach, so I took the liberty of having our dinner catered and brought here. We can go out onto the balcony. The food will be here very soon."

I stood up with Finn and followed them out through the left-hand tall, open window and stepped out onto a tiny balcony with a table set for three. The warm sea breeze brushed my face, and I thought I had died and gone to heaven. There was a bottle of champagne in the center next to crystal glasses with stark white bone china and linen napkins. This Adrien had style.

We heard a knock on the door as Adrien handed the bottle of champagne to Finn. "Agent McNally would you please do me the honor? I must answer the door and allow them to serve our food."

I waited for Adrien to leave us and I quickly looked at Finn. "Is this some kind of a dream? I feel as though I should be wearing an evening dress."

Finn grinned as he carefully twisted the wire around the cork and aimed it away from us. "I think I'd like to see you in an evening dress."

My face got warm as I heard the pop and watched the foam ooze down the bottle as he quickly poured the sparkling wine into our glasses. I tried to conceal my flushing cheeks and grabbed one of the tall crystal glasses and took a sip. The bubbles tickled my nose but the liquid smoothly dripped down my throat.

"Wow, this is amazing." I turned the bottle and

read *Champagne, France*. "This actually says 'Champagne, France'. I didn't realize there was such a place."

Adrien stepped back out onto the balcony and said, "Yes, many people get confused when they drink sparkling wine. They automatically call it champagne, however, this is not the case. It is only called champagne if it comes from the wine region in the northeast of France. This, as you Americans say, is the real McCoy."

I chuckled and suddenly felt carefree for the first time since I had landed at Charles De Gaulle. "It's delicious."

We watched two men and a woman wearing crisp white tunics and chef hats begin to serve us through the window as we sat down. Adrien placed his napkin on his lap and pointed to the first course being set on our plates.

"Our appetizer this evening is smoked salmon mousse piped on crostini, which is a toasted French bread. Enjoy."

I watched Finn make a strange face as he bit into the salmon. I think he was more comfortable in a pub setting, drinking a Guinness and eating a burger. He didn't choke on it, so I figured it was safe to try. The moment the salmon touched my tongue, my taste buds went into overdrive. It was amazing. I thought it was best to follow Adrien's lead as I watched him take a sip of champagne and bite into the appetizer. I continued to do the same and could have eaten the entire platter of salmon mousse.

When we had finished with the appetizer, the caterers removed our plates and champagne glasses and began to reset our place settings. A Pinot Noir was poured into wine glasses and then a beautifully prepared dish of roast duck and vegetables was placed in front of us. There were tiny roasted potatoes with tomatoes, eggplant and zucchini. I was beginning to wish I hadn't eaten so much salmon.

My knife melted into the duck, and when I took a bite, I caught Adrien watching my expression. I smiled and said, "I've never had roast duck, and this melts in my mouth."

Adrien winked and kissed his fingers and said, "*Magnifique*, I am glad you are enjoying your meal."

Finn took a bite and nodded. "I haven't eaten like this since I was in the restaurant Guy Savoy in Paris."

Adrien fluttered his hand over his heart and said, "That is my favorite restaurant. You give a very high compliment for our chefs. I'll be sure to tell them."

Once we had finished our main course, I was so full I thought I would explode. The sun was beginning to set, and I realized it had taken us almost an hour to get this far into the dinner. The conversation was light, and I frequently caught myself staring out at the sea as the waves crashed against the tiny beach.

Our dishes and glasses were again removed, and several types of cheeses, nuts, and baguettes on a cutting board were placed in the center, while they poured chardonnay into our glasses. I figured I'd play it safe and only eat a few nuts, which were complemented by the perfect white wine. I could feel my head getting fuzzy and decided to slow down on the drinking.

Finn grabbed some cheese and topped it onto a baguette and took a large bite. "So, tell me the history of this building. I know it was once a famous hotel."

"*Oui*, it was the Hotel Negresco, which was built

in 1912 and opened its doors in 1913. It was named after Henri Negresco. Henri faced a downturn when World War One broke out and the hotel was converted into a hospital. By the end of the war, the number of wealthy visitors to the Riviera had dropped off to the point that the hotel was in severe financial difficulty. Seized by creditors, the Negresco was sold to a Belgian company. Henri Negresco died a few years later in Paris at the age of fifty-two."

I finished my glass of wine only to have it dutifully refilled by one of the chefs. "How did it become a residence?"

"There are only twenty suites that are rented out for an extended stay. I have been here for two years. I will hate to leave when the time comes." Adrien finished his wine and waved his hand to the waiting chefs inside.

I glanced through the window and saw the chefs scurry, and then directed my attention back to Adrien. "How long have you been an agent?"

"I retired three years ago, but I have agreed to remain undercover when needed. I move about where they need me to set up and help other agents, such as in your case."

I watched the clearing of plates and glasses ritual and thought we had finished, until we were lavished with small dessert plates of little fruit tarts with blueberries, red raspberries and grapes atop yogurt cream, inside a tiny piecrust. How in the world could I resist this?

The sky had now turned a dark purple with the reflection of the moon as I carefully balanced the fruit on my fork and took a bite. It was out of this world. My pants no longer fit across my waist. I knew it would be rude not to finish the dessert, as well as un-button my jeans. I finished the last bite of the yogurt cream and almond pie crust and settled back against my chair.

"Adrien, I have to say this has been the best experience I've ever had eating dinner. I can't believe we've been out here for two and a half hours." I could feel the wine going to my head, and I gave him my lazy smile.

Finn raised his right eyebrow and said, "You do know that we have work to do after dinner?"

"What do you mean, work?"

Finn set down his fork and wiped his sexy mouth with the linen napkin. "I plan on going over to Dubsky's place to watch if there's any activity going on. You think you can stay awake?"

I watched the chefs remove our dessert plates, which were replaced with tiny coffee cups. They poured thick, hot espresso, and the pungent smell of coffee filled my nostrils. I suddenly felt rejuvenated and decided I would need the coffee to keep me awake.

"Absolutely, I won't have any problem, how about you?"

"This is my job. I'm used to it." Finn set down his empty cup and got up from his chair. "Adrien, this was a delight and we truly appreciate your hospitality. I'd like to use the *toilette*, and then we'll be on our way for a few hours. Are you sure you don't mind putting us up tonight?"

"Of course not. I have a guest room for Ms. Mills and a pullout sofa for you, if that is okay?"

Finn nodded and said, "That'll work just fine."

I guessed that I was finished with my coffee and

slowly got up from my chair. My legs had fallen asleep, and I figured I could use the bathroom as well. "Yes, that will be fine, and again, thank you for the amazing dinner. I'll cherish this night and your hospitality for a very long time."

After using the *toilette*, Finn and I met at the door and said our momentary good evenings to Adrien and headed toward the elevator. I couldn't breathe, and the coffee did nothing to help me remain awake. I entered the elevator and decided I would unbutton my pants when we got into the car. No harm, no foul.

"You seem quiet all of a sudden." Finn waited for me to exit the elevator and followed suit.

"I can't breathe after that amazing meal. I've never eaten like that before. Plus, I'm a bit sleepy. I thought the coffee would wake me up."

"Yes, the French know how to turn a meal into an event." Finn hit the fob and unlocked the car.

I slid into my seat and inconspicuously unbuttoned my jeans as my gut rolled out and pushed the zipper down. *Man, am I going on a diet when I return home.* "I don't think my pants fit anymore."

Finn chuckled and started the engine. "Buy new ones."

"Are you kidding me? Why do men think that's the answer? You don't buy new fat pants. You lose the weight to fit into your skinny pants."

"Sorry, didn't mean to hit a nerve."

I rolled my eyes and grabbed my camera to be at the ready. "So what are we looking for exactly at Dubsky's place?"

"Your niece for one, and anything else that looks suspicious."

We rolled up the hill at a snail's pace, and Finn

maneuvered the car above the house, so we had a clear view of the entire back pool and patio. The lights were on in the house, and you could clearly see people moving around.

I placed the camera against my eye as I adjusted the viewfinder and zoomed in and began taking pictures and whispered, "I can see two men carrying some pretty big guns."

Finn reached into the back seat and shuffled through his backpack, revealing binoculars. He put them up to his eyes. "I count three. I don't see Dubsky."

"How do you know what he looks like?" I continued to take pictures of the different men of all different shapes and sizes, who were coming and going behind the wall of windows.

"The agency sent me a picture of him. He's squat, fat and bald."

"Oh, lovely and his men are big, huge, and ugly." I continued to take pictures and suddenly I spotted Mandy briefly walk past the windows and then she went out of view as my voice caught in my throat.

Finn spoke before I could and said, "Is that Mandy?"

"It is! I can't believe it! She looks okay, at least from what I can see."

CHAPTER ELEVEN

My eyes remained frozen on the lens as I waited for Mandy to pop back into view. "Let's go get her."

Finn set the binoculars down on his lap and timidly looked at me. "Hannah, we can't just rush in there yet. I will need more backup. We need to plan this out methodically. Now that we know she is there, we'll be able to strategize our next move."

I couldn't believe my ears! I set the camera down and stared back at his emerald eyes. "Are you kidding me? We've come out here tonight, and we're not going to do anything now to get Mandy? What if they move her again? How long is it going to take to get help?"

"They won't move her."

"How do you know that? She's been moved twice so far. I'm not waiting." I'd started to jiggle the door handle when Finn grabbed my arm and pulled me back against the seat.

"Look, we'll have a team together by early morning. It's late, and you can tell they have no plans of leaving and besides..."

"Besides, what?"

"I think Mandy is here for Dubsky himself. He hasn't sold her off."

The tears began to spill out of my eyes and down my face. My ears started to ring, and I thought I would upchuck my entire fabulous dinner all over the car. "How do you know that for sure? I want to get her out of there."

Finn grabbed a napkin from the center console and handed it to me. "Hannah, we need to have a better plan than just rushing in. You can be sure they have a plan of evacuating her if something goes wrong. We need to go back to Adrien's, and we'll make a few phone calls. That's what he's here for. He's got local contacts. We won't have to wait long, I promise you."

I blew my nose and dropped my head against the seat. "You'd better be right, because if anything happens to her, I'll hold you responsible."

We drove back to Adrien's in silence. My head was pounding, and I felt like I had just run a marathon. I couldn't wait to plop my weary body down in Adrien's guest room bed. I wondered how much sleep I would actually get.

Once inside the apartment, Finn and Adrien began making calls. I told them I was going to bed but decided to take a shower first. Again, the shower and sink were separate from the *toilette*, which I thought was a neat concept.

I took my sweatpants and t-shirt into where the shower and sink were located and turned on the light. The counter and walls were a cinnamon marble. The sink was a clear green bowl, and the handles and faucet were square and stainless steel. To the right was a huge, claw-foot tub with a showerhead strategically placed on the edge against the wall.

I knew right then and there that I was going to take a nice long soak. I regulated the water and plugged the drain and began to fill the tub. There were scented soaps and gels on a shelf, and I chose lavender scent and dumped it into the water and watched the bubbles begin to form. The smell was fantastic and I couldn't wait for it to fill as I slipped down into the smooth cast iron and laid my head against the back.

I almost felt guilty lying here while Mandy was stuck with a squat, fat creep, not knowing if she'd ever see us again. I had to change my thoughts and think positive that Finn and Adrien were working on a plan. All that mattered to me was that she was alive. I wouldn't think about what may have happened to her being traded back and forth. I would have to put my faith in Finn.

I was able to reach a washcloth from the shelf, and I loaded it up with the lavender gel and washed my aching muscles. I found shampoo that smelled of peach and lathered my head and then held my breath and dropped below the water to rinse myself. I popped back up and wiped the water from my eyes. I felt sleepy and laid my head back again and started to drowse. Within a few seconds, though, my mind's eye had shifted to Finn's firm ass, and I quickly opened my eyes and tried to wipe that vision out of my head.

I smiled to myself and began to watch the water drip from the faucet, but in the stillness, the sound tapped out a rhythm that actually annoyed me, so I stuck my right big toe up the metal opening to stop the noise. It was a little awkward to remain in that position, so I realized it was time to finish this soak and dry off and tried to pull out my toe, but it wouldn't budge.

I scooted closer to the faucet and again tried to pull my toe out, but the more I struggled, the tighter the grip. I started to panic and grabbed some gel and tried to lather my toe, hoping it would loosen. Nothing; it only seemed to get worse. *What the hell was I going to do?* In an instant, the vision of one of the reruns of the *Dick Van Dyke Show* came to mind, of Laura Petrie getting her toe stuck. The only problem was I couldn't remember how they got it out.

I took a few deep breaths and tried to relax my foot, not quite sure how relaxing my foot would shrink my toe, but I was willing to try anything. It still wouldn't release. I finally took a deep breath and realized what I had to do. My clothes were on top of the sink, and the nearest towel was on a warming rack at the other end of the tub. I couldn't reach it.

I shook my head and then yelled, "Finn, could you please come to the door of the bathroom?"

Footsteps came to the door, and Finn replied, "Yes, what is it?"

"I have a bit of a problem and when I tell you what that problem is, do you think you can refrain from laughing?"

"I can try, but I won't promise you anything."

Great, this was all I needed, me sitting in here naked and him getting a big laugh out of it. I again tried to pull out my toe, but this time it hurt. "I got my big toe stuck in the tub faucet."

"Wait a minute, did you just say your toe is stuck in the faucet? How the hell did you do that?"

I could feel my heart beating faster and my face

getting hot. "I'm really not in the mood to go into an explanation. I can't reach my clothes or a towel, so I need you to be chivalrous and close your eyes and give me a towel so I can cover myself. Then you'll need to help me release my toe."

Finn said, "You'll need to drain the water. In the meantime, I'll see if Adrien has anything to grease up your toe."

"No, don't bother him. I'm embarrassed enough as it is." There was no sound outside the door, so I drained the water as he said, tried to sit as close against the wall of the tub, and then leaned forward to conceal my naked body. I tucked my arms around my legs and glanced at the washcloth, knowing full well that wasn't going to hide anything.

I heard a knock on the door and Adrien said, "Ms Mills, I have some coconut oil that may help you release your toe. I will give it to agent McNally. If this doesn't work, we may have to call the building maintenance man."

Oh Lord, I didn't want anyone else in here. I didn't even want Finn in here. I took a deep breath and said, "Okay, Finn, cover your eyes. I'll direct you to where the towel and my clothes are, and then I can try to cover myself."

Finn opened the door and slowly walked into the bathroom. "I've got my eyes closed."

"And no peeking."

"I'm not peeking. Just guide me to where I'm going."

"Okay, my clothes are on the sink, which is to your left. The towel is just to the right of that on a warming rack."

Finn carefully stepped toward his left and

reached out and down and found my clothes. He then moved carefully to his right and ran his hand against the wall until he touched the towel. He turned toward me and said, "Okay, start talking so I can walk over to you."

"I'm about four steps to your right." I stared at his eyes, making sure he kept them closed. "Okay, good, you're right above me. I'm going to reach up and grab the towel first, but keep your eyes closed."

Finn revealed his sexy smirk and said, "This hardly seems fair that I don't at least get the chance for a peek since I'm in here trying to help you out."

"Yeah, nice try."

I grabbed the towel and quickly rubbed my head and swiftly dried my upper body, which had started to get a chill. I then draped it around me from the front and tucked the ends under my ass. I quickly slid my nightshirt on and realized I couldn't put on my sweatpants. When I felt comfortable that I was covered, I said, "Okay, you can open your eyes."

Finn opened his eyes and immediately began to laugh. "This reminds me of something from television. I think I've seen this before."

"I don't find this in the least bit funny, and yes, it's from the *Dick Van Dyke Show*."

"That's right, and didn't they have to cut the pipe? I don't think Adrien is going to like that outcome."

Finn kneeled down and leaned on the tub and opened the jar of coconut oil. His eyes glanced up and down my body. "Let me see if some of this will work."

I grabbed the jar out of his hands and said, "I can

do this, thank you. Now, keep your eyes averted from staring at me, please."

Finn leaned back from the tub and nodded his head. "Very well, let me know if I need to ask Adrien to call maintenance."

"It had better work because it's bad enough you're in here with me. I don't need complete strangers gawking at me as well." I pushed my toe up as far as I could and began rubbing the coconut oil. It started to melt as I gently tried to pull my toe out. It wouldn't budge.

Finn stuck his finger in the jar and scooped out a glob of oil and then proceeded to rub more on my toe. "I think you need more oil than that and a little muscle to pull it out."

I tried to ignore all of the pulses taking place again in my pelvic region as his forearm rested on my thigh. Feeling his fingers rubbing the oil on my toe was about to put me over the edge. He carefully wiggled my toe a bit and then yanked my foot. My toe popped out, and I landed at the back of the tub. The towel had ridden up my thighs, exposing all of my glory as a huge grin fell on Finn's face.

My nipples got hard and were exposed through my shirt as I frantically shoved the towel back down to my knees. My face was hot as I tried to avoid looking into his eyes. "Thanks, can you please go now? I'd like to finish drying off and go to bed."

Finn stood up and winked. "Of course, although it hardly seems we're strangers anymore."

Before I could scream at him, he left the bathroom and closed the door behind him. I still wanted to scream but instead, I dropped my face into my hands and started to cry. I was mortified. I wiped the tears from my face and got out of the tub. My legs had fallen asleep, and my ass was numb. I grabbed my sweatpants and shoved them on and hurriedly brushed my teeth. I placed the towel back on the rack and tried to leave the bathroom as I found it, then grabbed my things and slowly opened the door.

Finn was waiting in the hall. "I wanted to let you know that Adrien and I have got a team ready and they'll meet us here tomorrow at half-past six."

I could see he was still wearing a smirk as I shifted my arms up against my chest and said, "That's great. I'll set my alarm."

"Very well, and Adrien will have a light breakfast ready for us at six."

Finn turned to leave, but I grabbed his elbow and said, "Thank you again for helping me. It was such a stupid thing to do. I'm not even sure how it happened. I also appreciate you being a gentleman throughout... everything."

He reached his hand up to my face and lightly rubbed my cheek with his knuckles. "You're very welcome. Now try and get some rest. It's a big day tomorrow."

"Goodnight, I'll see you in the morning." I turned to my right and headed into the bedroom. I shut the door and leaned my back against it, trying to breathe deep. My heart wouldn't stop pounding.

I walked over to the bed, dropped my things, and plopped down face-first into the pillows, which were plush and smelled of lavender. I pulled up the soft duvet under my chin and tried to keep from thinking about Finn's sexy body.

I had just started to close my eyes when I heard a soft knock at the door. Before I could answer, I saw the door open slightly, and the light from the hallway illuminated Finn's tall body. He quickly shut the door and, in an FBI stealth-like manner, landed at the side of my bed and began to drop his jeans.

My eyes were bulging out of my head, but I didn't say a word. I continued to stare as he dropped his form-fitted boxer briefs. There, staring back at me, was the same colossal bulge I'd recognized in the hotel room. He swiftly pulled back the duvet and gently dropped his muscular body on top of mine and began to kiss my forehead.

My entire body reacted to the soft touch of his lips as every nerve ending stood up at attention. I allowed him to slowly pull the t-shirt over my head and throw it on the floor. I couldn't wait any longer for him to remove my panties, so I yanked them down and struggled to kick them off my foot.

He began to move his kisses down to my neck as he whispered, "I have a confession to make."

I could barely get the words out of my mouth as my hands hungrily stroked his broad back and firm ass. "What would that be?"

He moved his lips to my cheek and said, "I peeked at you in the bathroom, and I couldn't get the vision of your gorgeous body out of my head."

I grabbed his face and pulled his lips to mine and allowed him to satisfy my needs at last. The tension had finally broken. Now at least I could take this memory with me to jail, because it was probably the last time I would ever have sex.

_____

I smelled coffee and abruptly sat up and noticed the empty side of the bed where Finn had been. I looked at my phone, which showed two minutes until it gave the sound of a bugle to wake me up. I hurriedly slipped on socks, sweatpants, and threw my sweatshirt over my head and tried to wipe the sleep from my eyes. I couldn't remove the smile from my face. Last night was the greatest night of sex that I'd ever had, which probably wasn't saying much.

Before I grabbed the doorknob, reality hit me. This was it. We were going to save Mandy! I couldn't believe I had traveled this far and finally found her. Then I remembered where I was headed when I returned to the States. How could I face my family? How was I going to survive in jail? I didn't know the first thing about it, other than having watched *Orange is the New Black*. I shook my head and rolled my eyes. I always do this to myself. *Let it go, Hannah... moving on.*

I walked out of the bedroom and headed toward the magnificent aroma of coffee and baked goods. I turned the corner, and there were six men huddled around a buffet table of food. I stopped short when Finn smiled, turned and waved me over.

"Good morning, Hannah, right on time. Allow me to introduce to you the agents who will be helping us take down Dubsky and bring back Mandy."

I listened as Finn introduced each man, all of whom looked the same. They were tall, muscular, lean, and fit, with FBI crew cuts, different ages, but the same. I smiled at each of them and then made my way over to the breakfast spread on table, which consisted of orange juice, fruit, muffins, bagels, and coffee. It reminded me of a buffet at a conference I once attended in DC.

I tried to keep my thoughts in the moment and poured a coffee, added my cream, and then chose a blueberry muffin. Before I could take a bite, Finn walked over to me and smiled. I raised my eyebrows and casually asked, "What's the plan? When do we head over to Dubsky's?"

Finn lost his smile and gave me a stern look. "*You* aren't going anywhere. *We* are heading out in twenty minutes."

I had already taken a chunk out of the muffin and tried to speak without choking, but then a blueberry hit my taste buds and I couldn't believe how amazing it tasted. The French do everything better with food.

I heard Finn clear his throat as I opened my eyes and tried to talk, while the blueberries slid around my tongue. "This is one amazing muffin. Sorry, what do you mean I'm not going with you? You're not going anywhere without me. Don't even start shaking your head. I have to go. I need her to see *me* there, not a bunch of strangers, and don't think because of last night you can order me around."

Finn held up his hand and guided me over to the corner of the room. "Hannah, it's too dangerous. This isn't some television show. These assholes have real guns. I'm not taking a chance on anything happening to you."

Before he finished the sentence, we both looked at each other and then looked away. I took a sip of coffee and then set the muffin and cup down. "Look, I get what you're saying, and I understand protocol. I'm also not stupid enough to interfere. I'll wait in the back seat. I just want to be there for Mandy. I want her to see a familiar face. Please, don't keep me back now. We've come this far."

Finn took in a deep breath and then ran his hand over the back of his neck. "Okay, you can come, but you will listen to every direction I give you. If you so much as breathe in the wrong direction, I'll shoot you myself."

I watched him walk away, and I chuckled to myself. I shoved the last piece of muffin in my mouth and then grabbed some fruit and headed toward the bathroom, where I quickly fluffed out my hair with hair paste and did my makeup. I finished the fruit, brushed my teeth, and then went back to the bedroom to change into my jeans and sweater. I found my camera and slipped the strap over my shoulder and met Finn and the crew cut gang in the hall.

Adrien appeared for the first time this morning and stood off to the side. He said his goodbyes and good lucks as we all left and made our way to the elevator. I suddenly realized I was standing in the middle of seven giants!

The elevator dinged on the ground floor, and we all waited for the doors to open. I walked out first and stood off to the side until Finn came out and nodded toward the door. He directed me to the back seat of our car, talked to a few of the agents, and then slipped his ear bud into his left ear and got into the car.

He turned and looked me dead in the eyes. "Hannah, I want you to promise me that you'll stay down and keep that damn camera out of sight."

I saluted him and saw no signs of a grin and said, "Okay, I promise. I'm going to stay right here. You won't even notice me." I made sure my fingers were crossed, which meant absolutely nothing, but it gave me a childlike satisfaction that I didn't tell a lie.

We followed two other nondescript vehicles out of the parking lot and made our way to Dubsky's. I stared out at the sea and made a promise that I'd take all that I deserved from robbing the bank, as long as Mandy was safe and no harm had come to her. Nothing else mattered.

It was now six-fifty in the morning, and the cars arrived at the end of the block in an orderly fashion and parked. Finn spoke orders into the air, giving directions to everyone listening and checked his weapon, holstered it on his waist, and then got out of the car.

I watched him adjust his weapon again as he zipped his FBI jacket over his bulletproof vest. He walked to the back of the car and opened the trunk. A minute later, he opened the back seat door and threw a vest at me.

"I want you to put that on. Do not, and I repeat, *do not* leave this vehicle. I don't care what you hear, you stay put. Do you understand?"

I slipped on the vest and fastened the Velcro straps. "I understand, but how am I supposed to know what's going on? How will I know when you have Mandy?"

"I'll bring her to you when everything is clear. Now, sit down in the seat and do nothing until you see me, understood?"

I nodded my head and slid down in the seat. I watched him close the front door and make his way with the other agents. I leaned against the front seat and peered over the headrest. The agents moved military-style, with weapons drawn, toward the house overlooking the sea. I said a quick prayer and sat back in the seat. *Please, bring back my Mandy safe and sound.*

I sat and waited for what felt like a whole lifetime when out of nowhere I heard gunshots. I sprang up and tried to see something through the front windshield. What was going on? The suspense was killing me. The gunfire had stopped, and again I sat in silence. I couldn't wait any longer. I grabbed my camera and had started to open the door when, off in the distance, I spotted Finn carrying Mandy in his arms. She was wearing a ton of makeup and a white silk sundress, while her hair was perfectly coiffed. It looked as if she was going to a party.

I flew out of the back seat and ran toward them. Mandy picked up her head, shoved her way out of Finn's arms, and began to sprint in my direction. We landed in each other's arms, and the emotions overcame us. We couldn't stop crying. I grabbed her face and watched the tears fall down her cheeks. I pulled her into me and held her shaking shoulders against my own.

She lifted her head and shakily said, "I knew you'd come for me. I just knew it. Oh, Aunt Hannah, I was scared to death. I didn't know if they were going to rape me or kill me."

I carefully pulled away and looked into her eyes. "You mean they didn't do anything to you?"

"No, they kept repeating something about *chistyy*. I don't know what it means, but they never laid a hand on me."

I heard Finn's voice say, "It means pure."

I looked up and said, "What does?"

"The word *chistyy* means pure. It means she

would have brought a much higher price for being a virgin. They must have been keeping her for the highest bidder."

Mandy said, "So that's why they had a doctor examine me! I wondered what that was for. So, because I'm a virgin, it kept me from being used?"

I pulled her back to me and said, "Thank God."

CHAPTER TWELVE

WITHIN MINUTES, THE AGENTS WALKED BACK TO the cars with five big thugs in handcuffs. I couldn't believe I finally had Mandy in my arms. I watched her expression turn to hate as the men who had held her captive for the last four days were being muscled into the agents' black SUVs.

I turned her face toward me and said, "It's time to go home now."

Mandy emphatically shook her head and grabbed me by my shoulders. "No, Aunt Hannah, we can't leave now. There were three other girls with me until last night. They took them to be sold. We have to save them. I've become good friends with them. Please don't let them be sold into prostitution."

Finn asked, "When were they taken?"

"I don't remember, early evening."

Finn looked at me and said, "We must have just missed them. Look, Mandy, I understand your concern, but we can't go around saving everyone from human trafficking. It's impossible. The plan was to get you back safe and sound. That's where it ends."

Mandy began to cry and dropped her head onto my shoulders. "Please, Aunt Hannah, please don't let them be sold. It's been horrific. What they do to the women is disgusting. I don't think I'll ever be able to erase what I've seen. We have to try at least and save them."

I gave Finn my *please can you do this one other thing* look. "They couldn't have gone far. Can't we at least give it a try to save them?"

Mandy abruptly lifted her head and placed her palms together and said, "Oh yes, please, please, let's try and save them. I heard the men say something about an eagle and that they were taking them to the port Côte d'Azur. I think that's close."

Finn stared at me while trying to ignore Mandy. "I need to get permission from my boss. This was only going as far as finding your niece."

Mandy glared at Finn, jutted out her chin, and slammed her fists on her hips. "My name is Mandy, and I've just been through hell and back. So if you're any kind of a real human being, you'll take the time to save these women."

Finn shook his head and ran his hand through his hair. "Great, I'm dealing with another pain in the ass. It must run in the family."

I started to chuckle and grabbed Mandy's arm to keep her from slapping Finn. "That's a yes, by the way."

"Really, he'll do it?"

"Yeah, he just likes to state his case, but if it means taking down more criminals, it's a feather in his cap."

I watched Finn talk on his cell phone as he paced

back and forth. It looked like a pretty heated conversation. He disconnected the call and glanced over at me with a look of frustration. He then turned his attention to the other agents and obviously began to share his plan. Within a few minutes, Finn walked back over to Mandy and me.

"I have no idea why I'm agreeing to do this, but I have a few agents coming along. We need to do this fast, and you two need to stay in the car when we arrive. It's about a forty-minute drive to get there, so if you need to use the *toilette*, now's the time to do so."

Mandy and I smiled, did a high five, and jumped back into the car. We, along with two other agents, made our way back to Adrien's and used the bathroom. I grabbed my suitcase, while Mandy grabbed some food left over from the buffet. Within fifteen minutes, we were back in the car, making our way to the port of Côte d'Azur.

Mandy and I caught up on everything that had taken place in the last four days as I tried to reassure her that it wasn't all her fault, even though I had those thoughts in the beginning. None of it mattered now. She was safe. We also agreed it was best for Adrien to make the phone call to my brother. Neither of us wanted to deal with that conversation and figured it would be best to save it for when we got back to the States. I also felt it was best not to tell Mandy about the bank robbery. She had been through enough and didn't need to have any more concerns added to her plate.

I caught Finn's eyes looking at me in the rear view mirror every once in a while. I wondered what was going through his head. Did he really mean it when he said that he didn't want anything to happen to me?

I knew I couldn't deny the attraction I held for him. I wondered if he felt the same way.

I brought my attention back to Mandy's incessant talking and listened to the horrific story of the disgusting jerks that sold women into prostitution. I remembered my camera and grabbed it from the seat and began to thumb through some of my photographs.

Mandy looked over my shoulder and said, "That was the first creep who held me captive. It was his nephew who took me from the bar in Hagerstown."

"He's in custody."

Mandy looked at me and then leaned her head back against the seat as tears began to drip down her cheeks. I grabbed her head and pulled her against me as I looked in the rear view mirror at Finn and mouthed the words, *thank you*.

I could see the port of Côte d'Azur come into our sights as we snaked our way down the highway. It was one of the most magnificent views I'd ever seen. Mandy had briefly fallen asleep and her head bounced off my shoulder. I carefully shook her awake and pointed out the window.

"We're almost there." I sat up and directed my attention to Finn. "How are we going to find these women?"

Finn caught my eyes in the rearview mirror. "Mandy mentioned something about an eagle. Our team was able to locate a cargo tanker by the name of *Eships Eagle*. It would make sense they would use a cargo ship to transport these women."

Mandy broke into the conversation and said, "You mean they've been put into one of those huge metal cargo containers? That's horrible!"

Finn replied, "Yes it is, and we've already contacted the local authorities and head of security at the port. We'll have plenty of backup when we arrive. We have no idea how big this operation is or how many men are involved on location."

We made our way down to the main road that ran along the coast. There were cruise and cargo ships everywhere, aligned along the port. Finn began to slow down as we tried to read the sides of each massive ship to see if we could find *Eships Eagle*. We weren't sure if we had the right information, but it was the only lead we had.

After driving for another ten minutes, I thought I spotted a large letter E coming into view, and as we made the turn, there in front of us were massive white letters displaying the name *Eships Eagle* on a cargo ship. There were huge cranes lifting and loading the metal cargo containers onto the deck. It looked like there were hundreds of these containers, which made finding these young women an almost impossible feat.

"There it is. How in the world are we going to know which container they're in?" I instinctively grabbed my camera and began to take pictures of the name.

Mandy stretched over to my side and looked out the window. "What do we do now?"

Finn talked into his ear bud to the other agents and gave directions to park along the side of the road. He turned off the car and looked back at us. "You two need to stay here. Let us do our jobs. We've made contact with the local authorities, and they'll be here shortly."

We both nodded silently at Finn and then looked at each other. I waited for Finn to move away from the car as I inconspicuously placed the camera against my eye and again began to take pictures of the crane dropping metal cargo containers on our ship.

Mandy quietly asked, "How will they know which container to look for? There must be hundreds of them."

I set the camera on my lap and said, "I don't know, but as Finn said, let them do their jobs."

Mandy bit her bottom lip, something she always did when she had either done something to piss off my brother, or was planning on doing something sneaky. "I can't handle waiting here like this. It's driving me crazy."

"Mandy, we've only been here for ten minutes, now relax. Don't go getting any crazy ideas and do something stupid. I lost you once. I won't lose you again."

Mandy let out a huge sigh and slammed back against the seat. She then turned and looked out the back window and instantly pointed toward the ship. "There's one of the guys I saw who came and took the women that were with me. Aunt Hannah, we have to tell someone. He'll know which container they're in."

She swiftly slid to the door and got out of the car. I jumped out after her and grabbed her elbow. "Where do you think you're going?"

"Where's agent Finn? Where is anyone? We need to tell them I recognize someone." Mandy pulled away from me and began to run toward the ramp of the ship.

I grabbed my camera from the seat and ran after her. "Mandy, wait up. We need to go together. Man, I wish I had one of those ear bud thingies, I could tell Finn what's going on."

We both instinctively ducked down as we made

our way up the ramp. As we reached the deck, I pulled her against the side and carefully looked around the corner. There was no one in sight. I waved for her to follow me and directed her to stay low and quiet.

We snuck between two of the metal containers and tried to stay out of sight. Mandy spotted one of the men who had abducted her go by at the other end of the container as she pointed for us to walk toward him.

As we made our way to the end, I held my hand up to stop, and I carefully took a peek around the wall of the container. There were four men carrying machine guns, directing women of every size, shape and color into the opening of another container.

I ducked back behind our container and held up my finger to my lips. I then took my camera and lifted the lens at the edge of the container and randomly began to take photos. I pulled it back and slipped the strap over my shoulder. Before I could say anything, I felt a hand grab my arm and yank me out from where I was standing and throw me onto the deck.

I unconsciously threw my camera at Mandy and screamed, "Run, Mandy, run now!"

I saw Mandy take off running and I prayed with all of my heart that nobody would find her. I then saw another man run after her as I stood up and started to kick the bozo who had thrown me on the deck. He yelled something in Russian and then slapped me hard against my cheek, which knocked me back down on the floor of the deck.

The other man, who had left, came back into view and walked over to me and laughed. I didn't see

Mandy anywhere. All I could do was hope she got away and went to find Finn. I looked up to the man standing over me as he glared at me with his gray beady eyes. He only looked to be as tall as me but seemed larger than life as he aimed a machine gun at me.

Another moron came up behind me and spoke in broken English. "Get up."

I turned my head and saw the third man, who was much taller with greasy, slicked back hair. He had a large scar across his right cheek, which looked as though he had been sliced with a knife. I slowly did as he instructed and got up on my feet. He then grabbed my arm and walked me toward the mouth of the cargo container.

When we arrived at the opening, inside were more than thirty women cowering in the corners, holding onto each other as they quietly sobbed. My heart leaped into my throat as I tried to struggle free. The lummox started to push me inside when, out of the corner of my eye, I spotted Finn on the other side of another container. He winked at me and within a few seconds, I saw him mouthing words into his ear bud.

Before I even stepped inside the dark, hot metal box, I heard voices yelling, *"Freeze, FBI!"* The guy who had me turned and I took my chance and shoved my elbow into his side and ran toward Finn. Guns were firing around my head as I met his hand and he shoved me behind the container. Once he knew I was safe, he took off running toward the men, who were shooting in all directions.

I balled up into a fetal position against the cold

metal and tried to keep my head covered by my hands. Suddenly, I felt someone behind me and I jolted in a panic, only to realize it was Mandy, sobbing, with tears running down her face.

I pulled her into my arms, and we both held onto each other, waiting for the gunfire to stop. After what felt like an eternity, the shooting ceased, and I lifted my head to check if it was safe to get up. We both stayed on our knees as we crawled to the end of the container and peeked out at the middle of the deck.

Agents had the traffickers lying face-down with their hands on their heads. I grabbed my camera from Mandy and had just started to take pictures of the arrest when I noticed the women slowly emerge from the other container. I moved my viewfinder and, in a frenzy, captured the confused looks of fear and relief on their faces.

They were from all walks of life, wearing clothes that were stained and torn. Some of the women had bruises on their faces and arms. I tried to keep my focus as the tears welled up into my eyes and then drifted down my cheeks.

Mandy pointed to some of the women, then she stood up and ran, yelling, "Adelina, Dominique, Marta, I promised I'd come for you."

I watched her fall into the three women's arms and they hugged each other with faint smiles and tear-stained faces. I felt like I was invading their privacy, so I placed the lens cap back on the camera and slung the strap over my shoulder.

I spotted Finn walking toward me with a twisted, stern face. I wasn't sure if he was going to yell at me for leaving the car, or throw handcuffs on me. He did neither. Instead, he cupped my face in his hands and planted a kiss on my lips. My emotions took over as I limply fell into his body and returned the kiss. It was obvious neither of us cared that the entire group of people around us were staring.

All of the nerve-endings in my body were tingling as Finn slowly removed his lips. I stared up into his eyes as he said, "Why the hell didn't you listen to me when I said to stay in the car?"

"I'm glad you didn't lead with that question first. I much prefer the kiss." I realized he wasn't laughing, so I shrugged my shoulders and said, "I couldn't help it. Mandy spotted one of the original men that abducted her, and we couldn't find any of you around. I mean, you didn't give me one of those ear bud thingies so I couldn't talk to you. We just thought we would be able to find where the women were."

"Do you realize you could have been abducted with those women, or worse... killed?"

"Yes, I'm fully aware of that, but in the heat of the moment it didn't matter. Besides, I'm fine. We're all fine."

Mandy slowly approached us and said, "Hey, I think there may be a better time to discuss your issues with each other."

I looked away from Finn and smiled at Mandy. "I agree, and this conversation is over anyway."

Finn blew out his chest and pinched the bridge of his nose, apparently trying to fend off a migraine. "The two of you need to go back to the car... now."

I rolled my eyes and turned away as Mandy followed suit. "Aunt Hannah, I didn't realize the two of you had a thing."

"We don't have a *thing*. I don't know what we

have." I stomped my way down the ramp and over to the car as my camera swayed against my hip.

Mandy wore a smirk and leaned against the car beside me. "From where I was standing, that was a pretty hot kiss. Did you two have sex?"

I placed my hands over my eyes and then ran them down my face. I could feel her eyes on me as I tried to find the right words. "Yes, yes, we had sex."

"And?"

"And what?"

"How was it?"

The heat began to run up my face as I tried to conceal my grin. "It was amazing."

Mandy let out a whoop and laughed as she draped her arm around my shoulders. "Good 'ole Aunt Hannah, it's about time you got laid."

"Hey now, stop talking like that." I smiled at her and shook my head. "Fat lot of good it's going to do me when I'm in jail." The minute the words left my mouth, I realized I let the cat out of the bag.

"Jail? What the hell do you mean, jail? Aunt Hannah, what are you talking about?"

I wanted to kick myself and wished I could rewind back thirty-seconds, but I figured it was time to fill her in on what I did back in Sharpsburg. After the long, detailed explanation, I watched her shoulders slump as she turned toward me with tears in her eyes.

"Aunt Hannah, you robbed a bank for me? I can't believe it. You would put yourself in danger to rescue me? Nobody has ever done anything like that before for me. How can I ever thank you?" She dropped her arms around me and squeezed me tight.

My head nestled against her neck as I whispered,

"Because you're my Mandy. I had no other choice. I didn't care what I did. I needed to get you back safe."

I don't remember how long we stood there in each other's arms, swaying and consoling one another, but the reality began to sink back in and it was at that moment I realized I had no desire to fly back to the States.

CHAPTER THIRTEEN

We all sat quietly in a row on the plane, wearing headphones and watching three different movies on the backs of the seats in front of us. Mandy had finally given up pleading with Finn to let me go. She tried every possible solution she could think of, but Finn continued to repeat that he had to turn me in. It was the law.

Finn and I hadn't spoken since our kiss, and I couldn't help but wonder if he felt anything for me. Was his silence because he, too, didn't want to turn me in? The plane was beginning its descent as the seatbelt sign came on and we were given the instructions to lock our trays and return our seats to the upright position.

I knew my brother, mother, and father would be waiting for us at the airport. I couldn't even begin to think what they would say. I wanted to disembark the plane at another gate, but that wasn't possible. I just had to pick up my bootstraps and take whatever I had coming to me.

I was glad, however, to have had the opportunity to submit my photos to an old acquaintance, Josh Ewing, who was a reporter at *USA Today* and fill him in on the human traffickers. I knew Finn wouldn't be happy about what I had done, but it really didn't matter much now. We took off before I received any response, but I had hoped he would run with the story. This type of crime needed to be stopped.

I tried to unblock my ears as the plane bounced to a landing and the engines roared as we glided to a stop. Mandy looked over at me and smiled and then grabbed my hand. No words were needed. I squeezed her hand back and gave her a wink. Message received.

Finn stood up and grabbed his duffle bag from the floor under the seat in front of him and slung it over his shoulder. Mandy had no bags to speak of, only the clothes on her back that Dubsky had given to her to wear. I reached up and retrieved my suitcase from the overhead compartment and followed the crowd in a single file.

Finn waited for me to walk in front of him. I suppose he needed to keep an eye on me in case I decided to run, which did cross my mind a few times. He still wouldn't make eye contact with me, which frustrated me, but I was grateful for him being an FBI agent. It was the only way we were able to get Mandy on the plane without a passport. Too bad it didn't get us first class seats.

I nodded and smiled at the captain and flight attendants, and again made my way out of the plane and through the passenger boarding bridge. I felt Finn's hand on my elbow, giving me the obvious sign not to try anything stupid. I glanced up at his face and faintly smiled... again, message received.

Mandy spotted my brother and parents and broke out into a run. She landed in Justin's arms and began to sob. My parents huddled around them, and at first didn't notice me, which I was utterly grateful for and hoped I could duck off to the side and sneak away.

Mandy lifted her head and pointed to me and said, "Daddy, you just have to speak with Agent Finn and tell him not to put Aunt Hannah in jail. She did everything to save me. Please, don't let him send her to jail. I couldn't live with myself."

That was the moment when my entire family turned and stared at me. I couldn't tell what they were thinking or feeling. My mother's face was long and drawn, with dark circles under her eyes, which were swollen from obvious days of crying. My father looked as though he had aged ten years, while my brother's face was hard to read.

Within a few seconds, all four of them surrounded me with hugs and kisses and words of concern and encouragement. Finn broke away and stood off to the side. I couldn't believe how amazing they were. None of them were mad, they were thrilled and grateful for the lengths I went to, to save their daughter and granddaughter.

After we had finished saying all we could say to each other, my dad broke away from us and walked over to Finn. I couldn't hear what was being said, but I know he was doing everything in his power to keep me from going to jail. What struck me as odd was that the both of them had small smiles on their faces and then shook hands. I had no idea what just transpired, but my heart started to pound in my chest.

My dad walked back over to us, and he tweaked my cheek. "We need to get back home, and Hannah needs to go with Agent McNally."

I said, "What did you two say, and why were you smiling?"

"Just a gentleman talking to another gentleman to take care of his daughter, that's all. We're free to leave. Mandy doesn't need to go through Customs." He then kissed me on the forehead and walked away.

My heart sank and I felt as if I would melt into a puddle. Justin gave me one last hug, as did Mandy and my mother. I watched them walk away, then turned to Finn and dropped my head. It was actually happening. I was actually going to jail. All of my hopes and thoughts of being released because of what I helped to uncover, didn't mean a thing.

Finn's cell phone rang as he nodded at me to walk with him. "This is my boss. Let me find out what we need to do next. We have a car waiting for us."

I rolled my suitcase behind me and walked alongside Finn. I couldn't make out the details of the conversation, but apparently, they were taking me into their field office in Baltimore. We made our way to Customs, and I ruffled through my purse to retrieve my driver's license and passport.

We had nothing to declare as Finn escorted me out the door and into a black SUV with two other agents. I didn't think I needed *that* much security! The driver looked the part of the usual agents I had dealt with in France, but the other agent was a woman. It was comforting in some odd way to have another woman in the car. As I slid into the back seat and waited for Finn to sit next to me, my email alert dinged. I had received a response from Josh, and the headline read, *A Ransomed Blanket Reveals Human and Drug Trafficking.*

I couldn't believe my eyes! There in front of me

was the article and photos that would be published in *USA Today* on tomorrow's front page. I wanted to let out a shout but decided to keep it to myself. Josh wanted to call and ask me more questions, but he knew I was in custody, so we decided to have our interview via email.

After finalizing the details, Josh explained that his editor was going to be making a phone call to the bureau. He wanted them to know the story would be published and ask if they had any comment. I figured the shit was going to hit the fan, but the story needed to be told, and I was well past the worry of what else they could do to me.

Finn looked over at me and said, "Why do you have a smug look on your face? Is there something amusing on your phone?"

I casually looked up from my phone and then looked him in the eyes. "No, there's nothing amusing, just interesting. So, what's the plan? What will happen to me? Will I be arrested, then booked? Do I get to make a phone call to my lawyer?"

Finn raised his right eyebrow and shook his head. "You've been watching too many *Blue Bloods* shows. My boss wants to talk with you; I really don't know what the plan is, although I did make it very clear that you helped us arrest two huge drug and human traffickers."

I thought I heard him wrong. Did he actually stand up for me to his boss? Maybe he actually *did* feel something for me. I couldn't find the right words to say, so I just smiled. Again, no words needed. I looked out the window and hoped beyond all hope that I wouldn't have to go to jail. Then I wished I hadn't just ruined my chances when they learned that it was me who sent the story to be published in one of the top newspapers in the country.

The stern, bulky driver made a left turn onto Lord Baltimore Drive and there on the right was an inconspicuous brown brick building with rows and rows of windows on all four floors. We approached the entrance and made our way to a parking spot. It looked harmless enough. I mean, I was happy they didn't have me in handcuffs or had taken away my phone.

Finn opened his door and said, "You can leave your luggage and purse in the car, as well as your phone."

I did as instructed and followed Mutt and Jeff toward the entrance, with Finn tagging behind. I thought it was peculiar that nobody talked to each other. It was almost as if they weren't allowed to fraternize with me. We went through the heavy glass doors and arrived at a security desk. Finn flashed his identification and then signed in a book. The man at the desk waved us through as we followed each other through a turnstile gate.

The hall was narrow. We passed several doors and then eventually made our way to a large, glass-enclosed office where an older man with gray hair and bushy eyebrows was on the phone. He looked up and waved Finn to enter.

Finn glanced at me and pointed to a chair along the wall. "Have a seat here and wait until I'm finished. Please try to make sure you stay out of trouble."

"What am I going to do? I mean, you can both clearly see me sitting here." I rolled my eyes and gave him a snotty smile. I was beginning to get tired of the cloak and dagger stuff.

Finn didn't say a word as he proceeded through the large glass door and sat down in front of the desk of the man I assumed was his boss. Bossman hung up the phone and started to talk to Finn. After a few minutes, his voice got louder, and he began to wave his hands in the air. Finn never moved. He only shook his head. At one point, Bossman looked out at me and then back at Finn. I realized the shit had hit the fan. He must have been on the phone with Josh's editor. I felt a little smug but tried to keep a smile from forming on my face.

Half an hour went by before Finn stood up and turned toward the door and left the office. His face was blank, but the blood had clearly gone from his neck to his forehead. He walked over to me, grabbed my elbow, and pulled me into a standing position. I decided to keep my mouth shut as I tried to stay in step with his six-foot-five stride. We made our way back out into the lobby, exited through the turnstile, and then made our way outside.

Finn released my elbow and pointed to the female agent who had been with us at the airport. "Agent Murphy will take you home."

I stood there with my mouth wide open and said, "What are you talking about?"

"You're free to go. Your stunt of sending those photos and your story to the newspaper worked. My boss got hammered from the powers-that-be to release you. They were getting all kind of heat about arresting you for a measly three thousand dollars."

"And apparently you don't agree? I don't understand you. I thought you liked me. I thought we had a *thing* going. Was our sleeping together just a whim for you? Do you do that often with female criminals?"

Finn's face turned red again as he started to pace back and forth and rubbed his hand through his hair. He stopped in mid-stride and turned toward me. "No, I do *not* do that with other female criminals, and please keep your voice down. In fact, I've never done that."

"Then why are you acting this way? Aren't you glad that I'm not being arrested? You sounded like you tried to convince your boss earlier about how much help I had been on the case."

Finn closed his eyes and drew in a deep breath. "I *am* glad, and I suspected this would be the outcome. What I'm pissed about is how you snuck behind my back and sent those photos to one of the largest newspapers in the country. What were you thinking, and why didn't you come to me first? Were you looking for the limelight?"

I could feel the rage building up inside me as I slammed my fists on my hips. "Listen here, Agent McNally, I just spent the worst four and a half days of my life trying to save Mandy's life. I robbed a local bank, which is completely out of character for me, flew to a foreign country scared out of my wits, never knowing if I was ever going to see her again. I had to deal with the likes of you and your co-agents and being treated like a third class citizen. Got threatened by a drug lord, got my damn toe stuck in a faucet, and then was held at gunpoint. Plus, I let you take advantage of me. So excuse me for feeling the need to share my story! Maybe I should have talked with you first, but you would never have allowed me to send the photos. I was pissed, tired, and afraid I was going to spend my life in jail."

"Only twenty years."

"What?"

"You would have only spent twenty years or less."

I closed my eyes and tried to keep the tears from falling down my face. "I need to get my car at the airport. Can Agent Murphy take me there?"

Finn slammed his hands into his pockets and nodded his head. "She's been instructed to take you wherever you need to go."

"Fine, thank you." I wanted to run into his arms and stay there permanently, but my stubbornness wouldn't allow it. I was angry that he'd never said anything about us making love or whether it had meant anything to him. "Have a nice life catching real criminals."

I turned and walked over to the black SUV and got into the front seat. I could feel him standing there staring at me, but I never looked back. As we pulled out of the parking lot, the tears finally released from my eyes. I was thrilled to be free and going home, but my heart ached for something that apparently would never be.

———

I smiled and stared at the job contract sitting in my hands. I couldn't believe the editor at *USA Today* offered me a job! I was going to be a staff photographer in their news division. My photos from the human trafficking story had received high accolades. I had finally arrived.

It had been two months since the *episode* in France. Mandy and I had gotten even closer, if that was possible. My brother and parents seemed to look at me in a whole new light, especially my mother. I had received many offers for my blanket, but I chose to do what I thought Great Aunt Dorothy would have wanted and donated it to the National Museum of the American Indian in Washington, DC. The brass plaque displayed our names as the donors. I think she would have been happy with my decision.

I had to decide where I was going to live, since I would be working in Tysons Corner, Virginia. Apartment hunting was a pain, but I found a sweet two-bedroom, one and a half bath in Idylwood, Virginia. The job started in three weeks, so I needed to finish packing and buy some new furniture.

As I was walking into the living room to grab another box, I heard a knock at the front door. I peeked out the window and didn't recognize the navy blue Nissan Altima. I opened the front door and there, standing in front of me, was Finn. My heart exploded in my chest as I tried to remain calm and aloof.

I nervously propped one foot on top of the other and said, "Finn, what brings you here?"

Finn was wearing a pale green polo shirt, which flattered his eyes, and skinny jeans. He folded his arms and leaned against the metal railing and flashed his sexy smile. "I came to see how the local hero was doing."

I tried not to smile but couldn't hold it back as I opened the door and said, "Why don't you come in?"

Finn followed me into the living room and stared at the boxes strewn all over the floor. "Going somewhere?"

I quickly picked up the newspapers from a recliner and offered him a seat as I sat down on my park bench sofa. "I'm moving to Idylwood, Virginia at the end of the week. I got a staff photographer position at *USA Today*."

Finn leaned back in the chair and crossed his left ankle over his right thigh. "Congratulations. It doesn't surprise me. The photos you captured of those women were Pulitzer Prize-worthy."

I felt all tingly again in my groin area and quickly crossed my legs. "Thank you, that's a very high compliment. So what brings you here?"

Finn awkwardly sat up in his chair and tried to do something with his hands and eventually he stood and looked out the window. "I've been thinking about you a lot since our last conversation."

I waited for more and then said, "And?"

"I never got the chance to answer you properly about my feelings toward you and what it meant to me that night after freeing your toe from the faucet."

"I see. So what is your answer?"

Finn turned around with his hands in his pockets and said, "You don't make it easy, do you?"

"Nope, and why should I? So, what's your answer?"

"I think I've fallen in love with you."

My heart stopped, and I could feel the emotions start to flood my eyes. I could sense his awkwardness about what to do next, so I stood up, walked over to him, and wrapped my arms around his waist. I looked up into his emerald eyes and smiled. "What the hell took you so long?"

Dear reader,

We hope you enjoyed reading *Point and Shoot for Your Life*. Please take a moment to leave a review, even if it's a short one. Your opinion is important to us.

Discover more books by Robin Murphy at https://www.nextchapter.pub/authors/robin-murphy

Want to know when one of our books is free or discounted? Join the newsletter at http://eepurl.com/bqqB3H

Best regards,

Robin Murphy and the Next Chapter Team

Point And Shoot For Your Life
ISBN: 978-4-86747-347-4
Mass Market

Published by
Next Chapter
1-60-20 Minami-Otsuka
170-0005 Toshima-Ku, Tokyo
+818035793528

19th May 2021